CUPID CURES

RETURN TO CUPID #5

SYLVIA MCDANIEL

VIRTUAL BOOKSELLER

Can Cupid Cure Not Only a Disease, But a Heart as Well?

Kyle Lawrence must fulfill a bet by dancing naked around the Cupid statue at midnight. Only he doesn't believe in the superstition of finding true love, and he doesn't have time for forever after. A beautiful investigator from the USDA has arrived to warn of a possible cattle epidemic.

Life has not been easy for Dr. Tempest Tangier. A no nonsense veterinarian, who arrives in Cupid to investigate the possibility of a deadly cattle disease. But when she shows up at the Lawrence clinic, only to see a naked man breaking in, she quickly realizes the town holds more secrets than her forbidden past.

Can a rigid doctor with a famous past and a veterinarian with a gentle heart rescue each other?

CHAPTER 1

"$\mathcal{T}$his is the craziest thing I ever remember doing," Kyle Lawrence, said as he tossed his pants over a bench. "Drew better not back out is all I've got to say."

Drew, their baby brother, a lawyer, had a big case going on in Dallas and promised to do the Cupid stupid dance another time.

Kyle stood shivering nude in the cold night air, laughing. His childhood best-friend, Cody had fooled them by tricking the three boys into making a foolish wager. Because they lost, here they were in the town square, while the rest of the sleepy village slept, as bare as the day they were born.

One heartbeat away from being arrested.

Besides, this was a ridiculous superstition. If dancing in the buff around a statue chanting some silly verse made a woman show up in your life you couldn't live without, he'd sell tickets. What were these people smoking?

At this moment, his life was complete, with his practice, his brothers and friends. Though the warmth of a soft woman curled around him at night was tempting. He was having too much fun to engage in drama, right now.

Women switched their feelings on and off like changing channels on the television.

Like his older brother Jim, he would keep his word, but when he completed his three laps, his empty bed awaited him. But sometime in the near future his impending brother-in-law would be the recipient of a payback. As the saying goes, 'Paybacks are hell.'

Now if only his worst nightmare for the town of Cupid, didn't come true. Soon as the results of the lab test came back, he would know what afflicted Cody's cow.

His friend stood off to the side grinning. "One minute till midnight."

"Our sister did this?" Jim said, disbelief tinging his voice.

Kelsey had a wild side, but the oldest, of the four siblings, Jim refused to acknowledge that little sister might be having more sex than him.

"Best night of my life," Cody said. "Picked her up running naked down the road."

Kyle chuckled to himself and avoided looking at his brother. If Cody was smart he would keep the rest of what happened that night between him and Kelsey. Especially if he wanted Jim to continue being his friend.

"I still think you tricked us," Jim said. "You knew she would say yes."

"No, I didn't. There were no guarantees she would agree to marry me and you guys almost screwed it up."

"Bet or no bet, I'm not running down a city street like this." Jim placed his hat strategically over his privates.

A chuckle escaped Kyle. The very idea of streaking down main street was something he'd never considered. Never and like Jim making a mad dash through the middle of town, sans clothing was the stuff of nightmares.

Standing there covering his junk with his hands trying to stay heated, Kyle reached his breaking point. Risking everything on what appeared to be a sure thing was crazy. Pure psycho nutti-ness and at any moment, their friend the sheriff could be driving up to arrest them.

Time to either do this or go home.

Glancing at his watch, Cody grinned at the two of them.

"Thirty seconds," he said.

What difference would it make whether they did this now or later. This dance meant nothing. This superstition had no bearing on his love life, his future wife or anything else. A nice warm bed called to him and the time had come to get this done.

"Screw this, I'm going," Kyle said. "The sooner we do this, the sooner we can put our clothes back on and leave."

Jogging around the boy in a diaper, the church bells began to chime the start of a new day. Why hadn't he brought his Stetson to cover his junk?

For weeks, this moment, like a stick in the eye had lingered until finally he decided to just do it so he could move on.

"Chant, you have to chant," Cody called out to them.

"Oh, Cupid-statue-find-us-our-true-love," Kyle said in a singsong way that showed exactly what he thought of doing this absurd silly wager. Only a jackass believed this was how you met a woman.

"Oh Cupid-statue-find-us-our-true-love," Jim said joining in.

A full moon shone down on the God of Love and now Kyle knew why Ryan suggested the city council should remove the sculptured rock from the town square. Water gurgled in the fountain and as a vet, he understood his manly bits could be prone to frostbite.

Running faster he only wanted to finish, put his clothes on and go home.

"Last lap," Kyle called as they sprinted past Cody.

"Soon you'll meet your true love" his friend said with a laugh.

Who cares. Right now, Kyle's focus was on receiving the results of the tests he sent off earlier this week after examining

Cody's heifer. Not since his days at school had he seen a case of what he suspected. And if the tests confirmed his suspicions, Cody would have more to worry about than the outcome from tonight's adventure.

Soon Kyle promised himself a couple of days resting on a beach. A few days laying in the sun, watching women walk by in bikinis sounded like an ideal vacation. Sun, sand and bikinis.

Suddenly Jim's voice rent the air. "Cody," he yelled. "You son--"

Coming around the fountain to where his clothes should have been on the bench, there was nothing. No jeans, no shirt, no belt, no shoes, no cell phone, no keys.

Rage roared through him at the realization, his friend, soon to be brother-in-law had left them high and dry.

"Come on, man," Kyle said, throwing his hands up. "Really? How could he leave us here bare ass naked?"

Shaking his head, Jim groaned. "I'm going to kick his butt the next time I see him. We ponied up. Nothing was said about making us run through town nude."

With a sigh, Kyle said, "I'm two blocks from the clinic."

Shivering, his brother motioned with his hand. "Come on, there's some coveralls and a spare key in the truck. All I have to do is punch in the lock code on the door. I'll drop you off."

"Let's get out of here before the sheriff shows up," Kyle agreed.

Before they stepped out of the park, he watched as Jim scanned the street looking for any police vehicles. All they needed was to be hauled in front of a judge for doing the naughty dance. While some people would cheer, others would deem them certifiable. And frankly, Kyle thought the later.

When they reached the safety of the vehicle, Jim unlocked the doors and Kyle jumped in. Dropping his straw hat on the seat, Kyle grabbed it.

"I'm borrowing your hat," he said, placing the straw hat over his twinkie while Jim yanked out the set of overalls in the back. Quickly, he pulled them up and over him.

"Keep it. It's yours."

"Don't mind if I do."

At least he had the vital parts shielded.

Hopping up inside the old farm truck Jim sighed. "Glad that madness is over."

Quivering with cold, sitting in the buff beside him, Kyle glared into the darkness.

"That sculpture has nothing to do with finding love. No matter what Cody says about him and Kelsey, running in your birthday suit around a chunk of granite is not going to find happiness. A warrant maybe. Take me to the clinic. There is going to be hell to pay when I find Cody Graham."

With a turn in the ignition, the old engine started, and Jim gave a nervous snort. The sheriff's car drove down the street behind them and they turned and stared at each other. Another five minutes and they would've been calling little brother Drew to bail them out of jail.

CHAPTER 2

*D*r. Tempest Tangier sat in the darkened parking lot, waiting for the sun to rise. Driving through Cupid, she noticed the only hotel in town the marquee sign said was closed for repairs. So instead of coming in tomorrow morning, she drove to the veterinary clinic and rang the bell. No answer.

Now here she sat hanging around for daylight to come with news that no veterinarian enjoyed hearing. Brucellosis. Or at least a suspected case of the venereal disease for cattle. An entire herd could be wiped out because some randy bull got the clap.

"Surely, there's another hotel in town," she said out loud searching on her phone, finding no results.

Sighing, she gazed out at the darkness. Someday she would own her own veterinarian hospital and could quit traipsing across the country telling ranchers, their cows had an illness that warranted the death of an animal or a rancher's herd quarantined. It was not a pleasant job, but a necessary one that paid the bills and kept a roof over her head.

A truck pulled into the lot where she waited. Lights flashed across her car and she slumped down further in the seat. With fascination she watched as a naked man, hopped out of the vehi-

6

cle. A worn cowboy hat covered his loins. But the rest of him bare assed as the day he came from his mother's womb.

A giggle escaped her lips as he strode towards the front door. And he wasn't bad looking. Tall, muscular with curly short hair that most women envied. Glasses that gave him the appearance of a professor. Shame that symbol of western men hid his manhood.

Reaching under the mat, he pulled out a key and the idea struck her. Why would the good doctor be picking a lock on the door? What if he was a homeless man or a robber breaking in to steal the clinics drugs or harm the animals. A shiver of fear spiraled through her. It was her duty to call the cops. Even though she hated dealing with officers.

Yanking her phone up from the console, she punched in 911.

"What's your emergency?"

"I'm calling to report a break-in."

"Location."

"The Lawrence Veterinary clinic and a naked man just went into the building?"

The man on the other end started laughing, startling Tempe. "Excuse me."

"Sorry, ma'am. The sheriff is on his way."

"Thank you," she said.

Less than five minutes later, a patrol car pulled into the parking lot. A man in a uniform with a gun hanging from his waist glanced over at her in the car. Strolling over to her, she rolled down the window.

"Did you call about a naked man breaking and entering?"

"Yes, sir."

"May I ask what you're doing sitting here?"

A lump filled her throat and she swallowed, her chest tightening. There was no reason to feel nervous, but every time she dealt with the law, she feared they would recognize her. "Doctor

Tempest Tangier from the USDA here to see doctor Jim Lawrence. Driving into town, the only hotel was closed."

"Yes, ma'am, a tornado took off the roof."

"Oh," she said. "Sorry to hear that. What about the naked man? When I rang the emergency bell no one answered."

"What did he look like?"

A blush flamed her face in the darkness. What should she say. All bronze muscles with a cowboy hat covering his privates?

"Curly sandy brown hair with glasses on."

The sheriff chuckled. "I'd lay odds, he did the Cupid dance."

"What?" She had no clue what he was saying. A dance? Naked? What kind of party required you attend not wearing clothes. The swingers club? Oh boy, this little town was rapidly becoming not her sort of place.

"Come with me," he said, opening her door. "My hunch is you witnessed Doctor Lawrence going in the building. Let's go check him out."

Crawling out of the car, grabbing her phone, in case she needed it. Her nerves jingled on high alert as she walked alongside the man, he chuckled to himself.

"I almost caught them."

What? What did he think he caught them doing. Maybe it was better that she stayed silent and let the law take the lead. No matter that she was innocent, she didn't need anyone scrutinizing her past.

The lawman pounded on the door and soon the same man, only this time wearing scrubs answered.

"Sheriff, what brings you here this time of night."

"Report of a burglary by a naked man. Is this the man you witnessed breaking in," he asked her.

"Yes," she said, thinking he looked even better fully clothed.

The man's brows raised and he glared at her. "Sorry, I work and live here."

"What was I supposed to think? You had no clothes on."

8

No one could reproach her for making the call. Any law abiding citizen would have done the same.

The sheriff started to laugh again. "Did you do the stupid Cupid dance?"

The man sighed. "Blame Cody. He tricked us. We lost a bet and had to dance around the Cupid fountain. No you won't find me dancing a second time."

Dancing? Naked around a fountain? Is that what people did for fun?

Shaking his head, the sheriff glanced at him. "You're just lucky I didn't catch you or you would have been looking out between metal bars."

Unable to keep silent any longer, she had to ask. "What kind of town is this? Dancing naked around a fountain?"

"We're a great little city, but we have some traditions that can get you arrested."

"Why were you waiting on me?" Kyle asked, gazing at her.

Tempe pulled her shoulders back and assumed her professional role. All this talk of being naked had gotten her off track. She was here to do her job.

"Dr. Tempest Tangier from the USDA. Are you Dr. Kyle Lawrence?"

"Yes." A frown crossed his face and he ran his hand through his hair. "Why are you here?"

"It's in regard to the test you sent us. I'm here to do my own investigation."

At this moment she refused to tell him anything more. All she needed was for him to decide not to help her get the samples she required for her job. In the year spent working for the government, she quickly learned not every rancher was elated when she arrived.

"Oh crap," he said shaking his head. "I don't think I'm happy to see you."

"Most people aren't."

CHAPTER 3

*K*yle stood staring at the woman doctor from the USDA. Everything he feared would happen seem to be coming true. The worst thing the old doctor from the USDA who use to come out occasionally and do an inspection must have retired. Now he had to deal with someone new. Oh no, this young woman not only was beautiful, but obviously had brains.

Beauty and brains a killer combination. And this woman seemed to have it all, looks and intelligence. A dangerous mixture that could be quite entertaining.

Shame she wasn't here on better terms. Because he didn't think for a moment, that she'd driven all this way to tell him carry on the test came out negative. No, the USDA didn't send out an agent, unless like a blip of trouble, you showed up on their radar.

"The cow came out positive," he asked.

"I'm here to conduct my own evaluation," she said, giving him a steady gaze.

Oh yeah, she was here to do her own assessment because that

old bull's sperm was in high demand, spreading venereal disease to every heifer injected.

"Right now would probably not be the time to go out there and start testing the ranchers cattle."

Her lips widened in a smile and her eyes twinkled, the green sparkling like emeralds n the light. "Didn't plan on chasing cows in the dark. If you men can tell me where I can find a hotel room, then we can call it a night."

The sheriff raised his brows at Kyle. Oh no, he didn't like his thinking. Sure he wanted to be a good guy and help the woman out, but that would be almost like sleeping with the enemy. She would be right here underfoot the entire time conducting her investigation.

How did he accept a government inspector here in the clinic making a decision on whether or not to put his friends and family's cattle down. He didn't want her here.

Ryan stared expectantly at him. "There are no hotel rooms within fifty miles."

"That's the next town," she said.

He nodded, his conscious pricking him. Well, crap, what choice did he have? Let her sleep in her car or drive almost an hour one way? But she needed to leave as soon as possible.

"My apartment over the clinic has two bedrooms and a bathroom. You're welcome to stay in the spare bedroom, here with me," he offered wanting her to say no.

She stared at him, her eyes narrowing. "Do you dance naked around this fountain often?"

Laughter rippled up from his chest and yet the thought of her watching him as he searched in the dark, bending over his buttocks shining in the moonlight brought heat to his face.

"No. I promise you and Ryan, that tonight was an anomaly. No more dancing around the fountain ever again. No more fumbling trying to find the key without my clothes desperately wanting to get inside the apartment."

"Shame," she said. "But the cowboy hat was an effective cover up."

Grinning only slightly embarrassed he said, "Gotta leave something to the imagination."

"If I don't stay, I'll be spending a lot of time on the highway."

"That's right," Kyle said almost hoping she said no.

"All right. Hopefully this won't take long."

Long as in how many cattle would be quarantined or long as in how many cattle would be put down. Either way, it seemed that trouble had rolled into town and would be lodging at his place.

CHAPTER 4

*T*empe had gone to bed that night, with a chair up
against the door to her bedroom. If Dr. Lawrence felt
the urge to go running naked through her room, he would find
the door blocked.

This morning she would examine a heifer that may or may
not be affected by the terrible Brucellosis infection. Learn which
bull in town inseminated her and how many cows he possibly
could have infected.

There were parts of her job she absolutely loved. Sticking her
hand up either the animal's ass or her vagina, not exactly why she
chose veterinarian medicine. And don't get her started on having
to put down any creature. Even a sickly cow was hard to let go,
when you knew a quick death was better than long drawn out
suffering.

Her love of the job was helping animals and saving them,
taking care of them, loving them. Not the part that ached when
she ended their life.

Dressed in her Levi's and her official shirt that proudly
proclaimed she was with the USDA, she fixed her make-up and
walked out the door.

"Good morning," Kyle said, looking up from his computer. "Rearranging my schedule for the day. Would you like some coffee?"

"Yes, please," she said. "Black."

"Oh, I bet you like it strong as well."

"What's the point in drinking it if it's not thick enough to give you a boost."

The rigorous days and nights of studying, she depended on caffeine to keep her awake. Glancing around the small apartment the walls were bare, no rugs, no pillows, no pictures. A hotel room had more personality than this small living space. Either he just moved in, there was no wife or girlfriend or only slept here and nothing else. The decorations were minimal,

The memory slipped through her defensive armor of the mansion where she once lived. Blocking the remembrance she turned and asked, "You live here long?"

"Since I bought the clinic," he said. "Dr. Greenwich and his son stayed here for a while, but he sold the practice and retired. When I heard he was selling, I jumped on the opportunity to own my own animal hospital."

"Nice," she said.

"What about you? How long have you worked for the USDA?"

"About a year. Right out of school," she said, taking the coffee cup from his hand.

A moment of awkward silence filled the room as she sank down on a bar stool around a counter that served as a table.

Placing his hand on his hip, his other hand holding his mug, he sighed. "Look, this is a buddy of mine we're going out to see today. He's marrying my sister and he's my best friend. His herd is just getting started and I don't want anything bad to happen to him."

"I'm not checking him out, I'm inspecting his sick cow."

"I know, but if you find that heifer has to be put down, won't you insist on putting down the rest of his herd?"

At this point there was no sense in speculating what could develop. Until she determined if the animal had the disease and the source of the infection, everything else didn't matter. First she needed to locate what she was dealing with.

"If the cattle are diseased, I have no choice. Government regulation number--"

"Stop, I'm aware of the rules. You don't need to recite them to me. But I will fight you, if you try to kill his herd."

"So his infected cows can infect other animals in the area and spread the disease to the supermarket? Is that what you want?" she asked, holding her ground trying to subtly make her argument.

Tempe followed the rules.

"Let's not jump to conclusions just yet. Let's investigate and see what we find," she said softly.

Charm boy would not keep her from doing her job. Regardless, he'd given her a place to sleep and some coffee. As an inspector, she was required by law to put down tainted animals.

He ran his hand through his hair. "Let's go. Let me do the talking. Let me tell him why you're here. Then, you can follow your government regulations."

"To the letter of the law," she said, standing up and grabbing her medical bag and her purse. Bad things happened when rules weren't obeyed. On their own, people made choices that hurt others, even their family.

"Of course," he said in a tone that clearly let her know, he didn't agree.

CHAPTER 5

*P*ulling into the drive, he saw Cody's truck parked under the awning. Hopefully he was in the barn and not out in the pasture working. As he turned the car off, he turned to toxic Tempe, the government watchdog. Like a pit bull - stubborn and dogmatic, determined to protect.

In the cab, she gazed at him, her emerald green eyes staring. "Look, I just want to tell you thanks for letting me stay the night. Hopefully today this will all be a false alarm and I'll be on my way back to Austin to fill out my reports."

"Yeah, let's hope so," he said, opening the door and stepping out.

Before they made it to the barn, Cody met them in the drive a grin the size of Texas on his face.

"The newest Cupid dasher has arrived. And did you meet someone? Did your sister deliver your clothes, your phone?"

Now was not the time to talk about this, but Cody didn't seem to catch on that something was wrong. Very wrong.

"Early this morning. You're still in the doghouse. Payback will be swift and certain. This lady called the sheriff on me last night."

Tempe stepped forward and offered her hand. "Doctor Tempe Tangier, from the USDA."

Cody frowned, shook her hand reluctantly and glanced at Kyle. "What's she doing here?"

This was one of those times when he wanted to spare his clients the bad news and couldn't. Nothing in school trained you for the first time you had to give a client a horrible diagnosis about either their pet or an animal they cared about.

"This has nothing to do with last night. When I got back to the clinic, Dr. Tangier was waiting on me. " He sighed, wishing this was not happening, desperately wishing not to his friend. "This is about the tests I sent off on your heifer. The one I told you to separate from the herd. You did do that?"

Nervously Cody wiped his hands on his jeans. "Yeah, she's here in the barn. After you were here last week, I kept hoping she'd get better. I thought maybe you were here to see her this morning."

"We are," Kyle said trusting his instincts that this cow was seriously ill. Praying anything else besides Brucellosis could be wrong with her, knowing instinctively the heifer would not live much longer.

"As a veterinarian with the USDA, I need to examine the heifer and run some of my own tests," Tempe said. "Do I have your permission?"

Cody glanced between her and Kyle and he witnessed the questions on his friend's face. "What's going on? Why are you here to inspect my cow."

Tempe sighed. "The blood work that Dr. Lawrence sent to the lab, shows possible Brucellosis. I'm here to conduct my own tests and make certain this heifer does not carry this disease."

His friend glanced at him, searching his face for answers. Now he had to deliver the bad news. The really bad news.

"Kyle, tell me what's going on. What happens if she's sick?"

This part he knew Cody would have a hard time with. The same part he struggled with.

"If she tests positive, she'll be put down. The rest of your herd will be placed in quarantine and we'll need to check them all to make certain they aren't also infected. This is highly contagious. When you called me, you said she was ailing and you didn't know why. Then when you said she kept losing her calves, I became suspicious and decided to do blood work."

"How long have you had this cow?" Doctor Tanzier asked.

"About three years," he said. "I bought her at auction."

The doctor nodded her head. "May I examine her?"

The realization of what this could do to his herd, settled over Cody and he tensed, his eyes widening and his shoulders pulling back. A stunned expression on his face, his mouth open in shock.

"Wait a minute. Do I understand this right? Quarantine my entire herd. I won't be able to sell them, move them? Take them to market? For how long?"

Tension filled Kyle like a bag of sand, heavy with a sinking feeling. No way would Cody like her answers. Already the man was starting to realize the effect on his herd, his livelihood, his ranch. Concern rippled across his face at the idea of all his cattle penned and taken to slaughter.

"You don't want this disease to spread to your neighbor's cattle, do you?"

"How do I know she didn't catch this from one of them? What kind of sickness is this?"

The doctor drew her shoulders back and looked him straight in the eye. "It's a venereal disease that is spread through fluids."

"But I use insemination. That's how she get's pregnant. She hasn't had anything to do with a bull."

Then he swallowed and threw back his head. "Oh crap. Ed Smith's bull got loose in my pasture. That SOB tore down the fence and there's no telling how many of my cows he impregnated."

"He's a champion," Kyle said in disbelief. "Ed demands big money for his sperm. He wasn't properly fenced?"

"No, he gets away from Ed," Cody said.

For just a second he wanted to find her blushing pink to the roots of her hairline at their frank discussion, Kyle glanced at Dr. Tempe. No, on the outside, she appeared unaffected. Her training was good.

"Well, I got it for free, unless he spread his disease among my cattle." Sighing, Cody turned on his heels walking towards the barn. "Come on, let's get this over with. How long before you learn the results?"

"I'll put a rush on the blood work, but at least two days. And she's been isolated from all other animals?"

"Well, she's been in a stall," he said as they walked into the building where he kept his horses and all his tack.

"If she's positive, we'll need to check all the animals," she said.

"Great just freaking great," Cody said he led her to the stall where the cow watched them with beady eyes.

"This is her," he said.

In sympathy, Kyle stared at the heifer and felt certain his hunch was correct. The animal appeared even weaker than she had when he drew the first blood sample several days ago.

Pulling on her gloves, Doctor Tempe stepped into the stall. "Okay gentleman, hold her while I do my job."

CHAPTER 6

*a*s they pulled back in front of the clinic, Tempe sighed as she glanced over at the rigid man sitting beside her. On the way back into town, they dropped the samples off at the post office sending them overnight. Now it was up to the results of the tests.

There was definitely something wrong with the cow, but she refused to come to any conclusions until she could read the report and verify the information. Soon, very soon they would know what they were dealing with.

In the meantime, Doctor Kyle Lawrence, was not happy with her.

"Now what?" he asked as he put the truck in park.

"Now we wait. I've got to write up some notes and send an email to my supervisor."

"Great, just great," he said, climbing out of the vehicle. "I'm going to work. I have a practice to run."

"Understandable," she said, walking beside him.

This was her dream. What she was working towards. To own her own hospital. The reason she had this stinking government job. It paid the bills, gave her some training in the profession, but it was only temporary.

Opening the door, the receptionist came running to him. "Thank goodness you're here. Mrs. Thomas dog has gone into labor and she's having trouble with the delivery."

A zing of awareness zipped along Tempe's spine. The call to help and heal radiated through her and she had to remind herself this was not her call.

"What room?"

"Two. And Doctor, she's been in labor for a while."

"Do you need some help?" Tempe asked, wanting to do what she loved. Itching to use her competence for good rather than bad.

"Sure, let's go," he said. "Why don't you let Belinda take you to the operating room and you can start scrubbing up. I'm going to calm my client and get our patient."

Excited, Tempe followed his employee into the room and quickly suited up in a surgical gown. Automatically her training kicked in and by the time Kyle came in carrying the poor exhausted mother dog, she was ready.

"While you scrub in, I'll prepare the patient for surgery," she told him.

For a moment, he gazed at her like he wasn't certain whether or not to trust her, but then he relented. "I won't be long. Don't start the anesthesia until I'm here."

"Yes, Doctor Lawrence," she said as she strapped down the helpless dog. Next she arranged all the tools they would need for the procedure, carefully laying them out. Last she put an intravenous line in the dog's leg to give her fluids. Everything was ready.

Joy at helping the mother dog filled her and she knew this was where she belonged, where she longed to be. If life had not ripped the rug, the foundation and roof over her head, out from under her, she would be running her own clinic at this moment.

Kyle appeared beside her. Looking at how she'd prepared for the surgery, he gave a nod in her direction. "Nice work, Doctor-Tangier."

They were back to that formal doctor language that let her know that he wasn't sure of her capabilities, but acknowledged she was a professional.

"Thank you," she said. "How do you want me to assist you?"

"Watch the monitors and take the puppies as I hand them to you. We need to do this quick before the anesthesia kills them."

"Of course." Excitement bubbled inside her, not because the animal was hurting, but the chance to help the mother. The chance to save her babies. The chance to use her skills.

"Okay, here we go," he said and gave the mother gas. Soon as she was under, he cut into her belly and soon had her uterus open. Placing his fingers inside, he removed the first puppy and handed it to Tempe. Immediately she began to clean the little dog's nose. The tiny animal squirmed in her hands, so fragile and precious.

Then the second dog, cutting the umbilical cord and handing it to her. For the next ten minutes, they worked in rhythm together, with him pulling the babies out and her resuscitating them.

"Is that all?"

He glanced at her, his fingers in the dogs womb. "I think that's it. I'm not finding anymore. Now let's save the mother."

Tempe monitored the mother dog as she swiped the amniotic fluid away and Kyle sewed the mother up. "No more puppies for this little momma."

Tempe peeked at him, still working on the last baby. "Does the owner know."

This animal didn't need to get pregnant again. Today the mother had a c-section, her uterine muscles would be weakened and a danger for her to carry another brood.

"She agreed to it before I brought the mother in. If she doesn't want to lose her, this dog shouldn't have another litter. So we made the decision to spade her."

"Wise choice."

"How many puppies?"

"Six, hungry healthy babies. Not even a runt among them that I can tell," she said, gazing at the tiny moving animals. Mewing and stretching and searching for a nipple, they would have to wait.

"Excellent," he said, taking a pair of clippers and tying off the last stitch. "Good as new." Picking up the syringe of pain medication and antibiotics he gave the mother dog a shot.

"Are you ready for me to give her oxygen?" she asked.

"Yes," he said.

Turning on the air, the mother began to move her head. "Come on momma, your babies are hungry. You've got a full time job ahead of you."

The dog's eyes fluttered open and she stared at Tempe, her heart swelling with relief. "Sweetie, it's all over and there are some sweet babies waiting for you."

When she looked over, Kyle stood watching her as he pulled his gloves off. "Why aren't you a veterinarian? It's obvious you love it. You did very well in here today."

So many reasons why she didn't have a vet business of her own. Mainly, money. The fact that it was difficult for her to get a loan, without answering concerning questions that would reveal her identity. Difficult because she feared someone in the financial industry would recognize her face. Hell, she was shocked so few people didn't call her out even now.

"I do love working with animals and being a vet. But starting a clinic takes a lot of money. So instead I work for the government."

Shaking his head, he smiled at her. "Good job, Dr. Tangier. We saved several lives today. I'm glad you were here to help."

"Me too," she said grinning back at him, her heart clenching at what they'd done together as a team. Saving the mother dog and her puppies made up for the lousy visit they had earlier.

"I better go tell her owner she's okay."

"Why don't I clean up while you're gone and then you can bring her back to show her the momma dog and her babies."

"My client would appreciate that."

"Give me a few moments to remove the blood."

Nodding his head, he stared at her with admiration in his eyes. "You really should have your own practice," he said. "You're an excellent vet."

"Thanks," she said and began to throw away the bloodied gauze. How could she respond? In the worst way, she wanted her own clinic. This was the goal. The very reason she lived.

Still the fear of someone learning her identity held her back in so many ways.

CHAPTER 7

*A*mazed at how well he and Dr. Tangier had worked together to save poor little Missy's life. The surgery a great end to a lousy day. Last time she had a difficult time, but not to the point she needed a c-section.

But this second litter one of the puppies was breach and larger than she could handle. This time they would have lost the mother dog and the babies. Losing any animal was tough, but especially a long time patient.

This time he told the owner, Missy didn't need to be having more puppies. The little dog couldn't do this again. And she agreed. Now, the momma was recovering with six babies to feed.

Reaching into the refrigerator he pulled out two beers. Tempe sat outside on the balcony checking her emails on her phone. Opening the sliding glass patio doors, he walked out onto the apartment's narrow balcony.

"Want a beer?"

A quick glance at him, he watched the way her emerald eyes twinkled in the light. A beautiful woman, but why did she have to hurt his friends. No, it wasn't her personally, and he recognized that. Putting aside his personal feelings for the good of the community, while remaining objective was hard. These were his family and friends.

"Thanks," she said, taking the bottle of alcohol from him.

Cody was like a brother.The loss of the cattle would be devastating. Though Tempe had nothing to do with the reason, except for being the bad news deliverer of the diagnosis. Brucellosis.

He needed to talk to Jim and make certain that the old bull hadn't gotten into any of their herd.

With a graceful plop he sank down on the swing beside her. A gentle breeze blew keeping the skeeters at bay as they listened to the early evening, night sounds and gazed at the stars glittering in the night sky.

"Are you going streaking again tonight?" she asked, not looking at him, but out at the lights in the distance.

After everything that happened today, last night seemed like a long time ago.

"Haven't decided. It seems like a nice enough night, but Ryan is probably sitting up there waiting for my brother Drew to do his Cupid stupid dance. We could go together. At midnight, strip down to your birthday suit and see what the God of love has in store for us."

Her brows rose over her rich, dark green eyes like she was warding off evil. "Look charm boy, that may work on some women, but it's not going to cut it with me.

Yeah, he didn't think so, but what did he have to lose. He'd been jesting, never planning on doing that stunt again.

"Never hurts to ask. Would hate for you to be left out."

"And why do you do this? What's in it for you besides frostbite or mosquito bites and the possibility of arrest?"

"Lost a wager to Cody. He bet with me and my brothers that Kelsey would agree to marry him and we didn't know they were dating. So we said that if she said yes, we would do the Cupid stupid dance."

With a shrug of her shoulders, he wondered how much she

understood about the superstition, but he would never tip her off. Because she was the first woman he laid eyes on after running around the statue. The realization sunk in and he shook his head.

Sure, Kelsey and Cody believed they were together because of her streaking and fell in love because of that night. But Kyle and his brothers, had no intention of searching for forever after. Who bought into such nonsense?

None of them would be influenced by the belief that dancing naked around the Cupid statue, found them the woman of their dreams. This was why he didn't believe in silly superstitions. The stuff of legends. Hocus pocus, mumbo jumbo.

The tale was a legend in the small town, nothing more. While the good doctor was beautiful, smart and quite capable, that didn't mean they would spend the rest of their lives together. He knew so little about her.

"What made you become a veterinarian," she asked.

A positive factor, they were in the same profession. Yet, she worked for the government. Nuff said.

"Loved animals," he replied, the memory of his early years on the ranch with his brothers and his mother and father. Those days had been the best. "Grew up on a ranch not far from here and we had all kinds of animals. Loved working with them, helping to cure them. Seemed like something I enjoyed and would never have to leave the little town I love. What about yourself?"

A deep, throaty laugh came from her. "Same. My school guidance counselor said I was intelligent enough to go into medicine. Compared to veterinary medicine that's easy. This is more challenging."

"Didn't you find the curriculum, demanding?"

Becoming an animal doctor was the hardest program in school, but somehow he managed to get through and graduate with honors.

"Definitely. One of my professors was determined to show me that a woman shouldn't be a vet, but I proved him wrong."

"Oh, there were always teachers who tried to weed out the weaker students. Those you learned as long as you held your ground with them, you were okay."

"True. Makes me even stronger, when they tell me, I can't do it."

"You are a stubborn person."

In the day they'd spent together, he witnessed her strong, stubborn side that lived by the rules. Yet she had also been the most thorough, meticulous vet to ever assist him in surgery.

"I am."

"How long are you going to work for the USDA? Seems a waste."

Lifting the beer bottle to her lips, she regarded him. "As long as necessary."

What did he expect? An honest answer? Perhaps she didn't feel comfortable enough to tell him the truth about her plans for the future. After watching her today, she needed her own clinic.

"How soon do you think before this is over?"

"Oh, you're ready for me to leave already?"

This evening sitting out on the balcony he enjoyed her company, but still the results of today hung between them. In some ways he could hear the tick tock of a ticking bomb in the background just waiting to explode.

"No, I enjoy having a top notch veterinarian here to help with emergencies. What I don't enjoy is having some bureaucracy tell me I've got to put down my best friends herd."

"Maybe it won't come to that."

"Maybe," he said. "Maybe the sun won't rise tomorrow or the moon tonight."

Lifting the bottle, he took a swig and gazed out at the twinkling lights of the little town he loved, knowing they had no idea of what was possibly spreading in the cattle.

"Oh no, not the moon," she said, her voice tinged with sarcasm. "I like looking up and seeing him smiling down on me. Check him out sometime."

Turning towards her in the swing, a strong surge of awareness flowed over him. Sitting outside in the moonlight, after a day of highs and lows a feeling of contentment came over him. Gazing at Tempe in the darkness, the urge to get under her skin, rattle the confident woman overcame him.

"The only time I need moon rays is when I'm courting a girl. I like to pull her in close, like this," he said, pulling Tempest on the swing, wrapping his arm around her. "Then I lean in and deeply inhale her perfume and think my oh my she smells wonderful. I let my lips linger on her ear lobe, letting my breath tickle the side of her neck."

Surprising, Tempest didn't move and she smelled like heaven. In fact, she'd frozen with his arms around her. "Then I move my mouth hovering right above hers, before I swoop in for a kiss."

For some reason he didn't understand, he wanted to kiss her. Layer his mouth over hers and drink from her lips like he was desperate for water.

Without stopping, he covered her lips with his, tasting the beer on her, enjoying the fullness of her mouth, the way she fit against him.

A zing of need spiraled through him and like standing in front of a speeding bullet, this could only be trouble. Oh no, she was the enemy. He had to remember the havoc this woman could inflict on the people he cared about, but damn she tasted so delightful.

Slowly he released her lips and stared down at her, uncertain as to who was more shocked. She appeared cool and collected, while he felt like someone had just slammed into him, knocking the breath out of him. Not wanting her to see how much that kiss affected him, he went for sarcasm.

"And that's how I use the moon."

Her eyes opened, narrowing at him as she leaned back and laid her head against the cushion. "I'm sure a lot of women fall for it, charm boy. But not me."

Stunned, he sat back and looked at her in surprise. No reaction to his kiss? No pounding heart or constricting lungs? No racing pulse or desire surging through her loins? Was he the only one sitting her reeling from the after effects?

Had he lost his touch?

Picking up her beer he noticed her hand trembling and then he started laughing out loud. Oh yeah, she felt the connection. She could deny the sparks all she wanted, not only to him, but to herself, but her soft, firm lips left a definite impression.

"You're right a lot of women do fall for it. Glad we got that out of the way."

"Me too," she said.

CHAPTER 8

*W*hen Tempest walked into the Braxton family restaurant she gazed at the decor. Just inside sat a bubbling water display with the man in the diaper aiming his arrow straight at you. Though the town was named Cupid, several times she'd overheard talk of the fountain in the square. What was going on with this statue? Did she really want to know?

"Hello Kyle," Taylor said. "Great to see you. Who is this?"

"This is Dr. Tempe Tangier."

"Nice to meet you. Are you a veterinarian?"

"Yes, I'm a vet, but I work for the USDA."

"Come on you two, everyone is here, there's room at the table for the two of you," Taylor said, leading them through the busy diner.

Tempe turned to give Kyle an examining glance. If the tests came back positive, she would be the most disliked person in town for delivering bad news. That's why she avoided socializing with the locals. "Are you sure?"

"What? Oh come on," Kyle said. "This is the whole gang."

Walking towards the group, Tempe frowned. Just what she

didn't need to do, fraternize with people on a social basis who could possibly be harmed by her decisions. "This is not a good idea and I don't think I should. I'll wait for you out in the car."

"No. No choice," he whispered in her ear, his breath sending a delicious little shiver down her spine.

With a sigh, they arrived at the table and she smiled at his friends, jealous of the his life with family and friendships, knowing the demands of her job might not be in their favor. Even now, Cody Graham glared at her and she gave him a smile.

How difficult must it be for him to remain quiet about his problem and yet be friendly to her at a public gathering. For this reason and others, she never became friends with the people in her investigations.

"Let me introduce you to everyone," Kyle said.

"This is Meghan and Max Vandenburg who are expecting their first child. Kelsey, my sister and her fiancée Cody Graham who you know. Ryan Jones, the sheriff who you met the other night."

Shaking hands with his friends she noticed Kelsey seemed a little cool. Since Cody was her fiance that was to be expected. How many sitting here understood her reason for being in town. What had they been told?

"Jim and Kyle did the stupid Cupid dance night before last."

The people around the table laughed and Tempe leaned into Kyle. "Dancing naked has been brought up several times. What is the significance of this dance?"

"I'll tell you later," he said softly avoiding her gaze.

None of them acted surprised the brothers danced nude around a decorative bubbler in the middle of town and she found this odd. Actually kind of creepy.

"Where's Jim?"

"Just missed him," Taylor said. "He and Shadow had to run some errands."

"Shadow? That's her name ?" Kyle asked, glancing at each one.

"Jim rescued her night before last," Kelsey said with a smile. "Did you meet Tempe last night?"

Ryan started laughing. "Yes, we got a call that a nude man was breaking into the clinic. Guess who called and who was the perp?"

Everyone at the table chuckled while Kyle went silent. Confusion swept over Tempe, why the snickers? It had something to do with Kyle dancing around the God of Love, but what was the sense of acting like a fool?

"I thought maybe a homeless person was entering to steal drugs."

This produced even more laughter and she observed his friends questioning what she didn't understand. "What is going on? All of you seem to think this is acceptable behavior."

Kelsey's eyes widened as she stared at Kyle an incredulous look on her face. "You haven't told her?"

"Of course not. Why would I tell her when I don't believe in this silly legend. She probably would jump back in her car and drive out of town."

Cody smiled and she knew he would be happy with her pulling out of town But it wasn't going to happen. Regulations must be followed and in the end the rules saved many cows.

The auburn haired woman, tilted her head at her sideways. "So Kyle hasn't told you the importance of the Cupid dance?"

"No," Tempest said, curious how many sitting at the table had taken part in this strange act. "Anyone else here done this nude dancing?"

Snickers came from the table and she peeked at Kyle, who looked everywhere in the cafe, but at her.

Meghan laughed. "Oh honey, Taylor, Kelsey, and myself have found love because we danced. We have a superstition in our town that if you dance naked at midnight around the fountain in the square, the next person you see is your true love."

Turning to stare at the vet, she'd come to admire, unable to believe that a man of his intelligence, a man of science believed in such nonsense refused to look at her. "And you accepted this craziness and was naked in the town square?"

Finally, he turned his dark brown eyes on her. "Remember, I lost a bet and thanks to Cody, to keep my word, I had to dance around the statue. But that doesn't mean I accept this as fact."

Tempe's analytical mind was having a hard time grasping why anyone would condone such craziness. "The rest of you believe in this superstition?"

Slowly they nodded their heads. The curly blonde, Meghan, appeared to be the most outspoken amongst them smiled. "All of us are in the process of marrying or have already married because of the Cupid legend. Max was the first person I saw after I danced in the town square. Ryan almost arrested Taylor and Cody picked up Kelsey running down the road."

"Nice," Tempe said, wondering how many others in town claimed this weird practice and why would you admit to it.

"Now you were Kyle's first," Meghan said smiling.

The realization that they all supposed she and Kyle were a couple slammed into her. They thought he was her true love.

Helpless to stop herself laughter bubbled up inside and spilled out. If only they recognized her face, they would be running and pulling poor Kyle away from her. She wasn't searching for love. Hell, she wasn't even interested in finding a man. Life had dealt her a blow that would make it impossible for her to ever have a normal life.

The only goal achievable for her was to open up a Veterinary hospital, not find happiness with another person, dragging them into her troublesome life.

"What's so funny?" Kyle asked, his expression one of hurt.

"All of you believe in this foolishness," Tempe said. "It's not real."

Sighing, she could see him visibly relax and knew he feared her reaction when she learned she was the first.

"I'm with you on this."

The couples all glanced at one another and smiled. Meghan laughed. "We weren't believers either until we fell in love."

All she could think was not happening. Not today, tomorrow or anytime soon.

"Absolutely not," she said. "Once my investigation is complete, I'll be returning to Austin. My work comes first. The government doesn't pay me to find love."

The memory of him kissing her overcame her and she could feel her cheeks blossoming. Oh no, that kiss had been nice. Really nice. Like the best kiss ever, but she denied to acknowledge the attraction.

"Fight it all you want to, but you were Kyle's first. So far Cupid has been winning with all of us. Cupid three, resistance zero."

Fidgeting in his chair, looking away Kyle, seemed nervous. The charmer looked scared and that didn't bode well. What he didn't know was he didn't have to worry.

Once he found out she was Scott Gaston's daughter, he'd be running fully clothed as fast as he could away from her.

CHAPTER 9

The cell phone at Kyle's waist jingled and he glanced down and walked away from the table. Right now, this call seemed like a lifeline. Hearing Meghan tell Tempe about the Cupid superstition put him on the spot. As a doctor, he didn't believe in such nonsense.

"Dr. Lawrence," he said.

"Doctor it's, Gloria. Joe McBowen called and has a constipated cow and needs help."

"Tell him we're on our way," he said, thinking Tempe would need to go with him and assist.

Before he reached the table, he sighed releasing the tension he'd been holding. Relief at escaping the restaurant and the wolves sitting around the table. For a moment, guilt gripped him for walking away. For leaving Tempe alone, though she could handle her own. The temporary reprieve gave him a moment to regroup. When told according to legend that she was his true love, the woman actually laughed.

Kyle worried as soon as they reached the car, she would be interrogating him. For a second he worried Tempe thought they were meant for each other. No matter what his friends said, a statue was not dictating his life. Mumbo jumbo, he didn't fall for that stuff.

Instead, she'd laughed like that was the most ridiculous thing ever. Part of him felt relieved and the other insulted. After all, he was a great catch.

Reaching the table, he pulled Tempe's chair back. "Gotta go folks. Duty calls."

"Don't forget my party Friday night at Valentino's Bar," Meghan said. "I'll be disappointed if you don't show up."

"We'll be there," Kyle said.

"You'll be there," Tempe said, rising. "Nice to meet all of you. Don't count on me being Kyle's true love. The reason I'm here is my job nothing more."

All that earned her was a bunch of smirks and chuckles.

"Come on, we have an animal needing us," Kyle said, taking her by the elbow.

Walking towards the door, she looked at him. "What's the hurry?"

"Constipated cow," he said. "We're going in."

"Oh, my favorite," she said sarcastically and he couldn't agree more.

As she climbed into the truck, she stared at him an expression of concern on her pretty face. "Do you believe in this Cupid superstition?"

"No, and that's why I never said anything about it. It was bad enough, you witnessed me in my birthday suit, but for me to tell you, you're the one. You would never have stayed the night and driven out of town without looking back with no place to stay. They're all happy, but I just did it to appease a stupid bet I made."

Like she still couldn't accept the concept of dancing naked, she shook her head and smiled. "Good to know. If you deemed a piece of granite could find you love, then I would doubt your intellectual skills."

"My skills are fine," he said a little sharper than he intended.

"My parents were happily wed for many, many years and when we lost my dad to cancer, it devastated my mother. Someday, I want that kind of marriage, but I'm waiting until the right person comes along. Not because of some silly hocus pocus tale."

It was true, he wanted to marry and have kids, but not with the wrong woman. His buddies from college had raced to the altar taking the next step in life and now some of them are going through painful divorces. Not a goal for him. For him marriage was a one time option with the right woman.

"For a moment, I feared you weren't as smart as I thought."

A chuckle escaped from his lips. No one questioned his intelligence. "Nope. Don't worry about being the first woman I saw. That chunk of rock shaped in a boy with an arrow is not a matchmaker."

Bouncing along the dirt road they headed to the Ketchum ranch. "Lucky for you. I'm bad luck. Really bad luck."

Unable to stop himself, he glanced at her surprised to hear her say something so shocking. "Why?"

"My family is crazy."

"How is that?" he asked. "Crazy can mean a whole lot of different things?"

"Ever heard of Scott Gaston?"

A tingle of something ominous trickled down his spine. All of America knew Scott Gaston. The biggest swindler in history who had stolen millions from little old ladies, teachers' retirement funds and almost every pension in the United States. The man's investment firm had been nothing but a Ponzi scheme until the feds took it down.

"Of course," he said.

"He's my father. I changed my name to avoid the public humiliation of what my father had done."

Shocked Kyle almost ran off the road.

CHAPTER 10

Shocked Tempe sat there wondering why she'd told Kyle about her father. At this point in time he was the only person she ever told about her past.

The government seized all of their assets, leaving them penniless and her mother committed suicide from the shame of being broke and her father's infidelity. After her mother died, she changed her name, and moved on with her life.

"Go ahead, say it," she said, waiting for the shoe to drop. It usually did whenever she revealed the biggest financial crook of their time was her father. Quickly she learned never to mention him to anyone, until now.

She hated her father. She hated what he'd done to so many people affecting not only his life, but everyone around them. In fact, she moved from New Hampshire to Austin just so people wouldn't find her.

"What?"

"How did he get away with it? People including the FBI want me to tell them how he kept what he did a secret for so long. Believe me if I knew, I would have turned him in."

When the story began to break, her father set them down and

told them he was experiencing a little trouble, but didn't think it would harm them. Right up until the day they arrested him, he conned them, assuring them over and over that everything would be okay.

Kyle laughed. "Even if you told me I wouldn't know what to do with the information. My only curiosity is how this affected you."

A cramp roiled through her stomach remembering those turbulent times. "The first inclination I had that something was wrong, was when the boarding school I attended sent me home. I didn't understand what I had done to be expelled. Every semester, I made the dean's list. Later, I found out they'd not received payment for three months and the head mistress lost all her retirement money in my father's Ponzi scheme."

The memory of packing her bags while her snobby fellow students came by saying how sad they were she was going. After the trial, they wouldn't acknowledge her on the street. But, they didn't mind talking to the press and revealing they went to school with me.

The vehicle hit a deep pothole in the road, sending them bouncing on the seats. "Not until the trial, did we realize the depth of dad's deception. We had no money. No place to live, no car to drive, we had nothing. Even colleges denied me because they were afraid of bad publicity."

The cab of the truck was silent, before he finally asked, "What did you do?"

"Mom inherited some money years ago that she kept separate from Dad's account. After mom's death, I basically went to college on her inheritance. Her attorney helped me change my name and start my life over. In the space of about three years, I lost wealth, my father, and my mother. My way of life was over. I had to learn how to survive."

The most desperate time of her life occurred before she turned twenty-one. Anything she dealt with now, would be small potatoes compared to the world thinking your family and you are monsters. "How do you convince people you knew nothing when they want someone, anyone to blame?"

"You can't. What about your extended family? Did you lose them as well?"

Before they came around all the time, seeking favors, looking for money for tuition, a wedding, a funeral. But when her father became bad news they no longer were there. Not even to help her with her mother's burial service. Not one came out of fear of the press, leaving Tempe to grieve alone.

"Mostly, I don't hear from them very often. They don't want to be too closely associated. And I don't want to spend time with them, because I don't want people to associate the Gaston name with Tangier."

The road went from pavement to gravel and soon nothing but dirt.

"When it rains, I bet it's easy to become stuck out here," she said, realizing how this road represented her life. So many potholes, so many ruts, so many challenges. The first eighteen years had been smooth sailing and then three nightmarish years.

"It's safer to stay home until the mud dries out enough, you don't get bogged down," he said. "Do you ever see your father?"

Like a vise her chest tightened and she clenched her fists. Hell would have a blizzard before she would visit her father in prison.

A sarcastic laugh spilled from her lips. "Oh no. The lawyer advised against me seeing him after I adopted my new name. After my mother ended her life, broken hearted that the man she loved had not only stolen money, but cheated on her with a long lasting affair with a broker, she killed herself. I refused to see him again. Scott Gaston is dead to me."

Occasionally, there would be something on television about him, but frankly, she would never see him again. Life had totally transformed and upended her while she was making it on her own. The scandal and heartbreak were unforgettable.

For her own peace of mind and sanity, she forgave him, but she would never have anything to do with him.

"What will you tell your children about him?" he asked.

This hurt the most. How could she bring innocent people into her life that at any moment could become unhinged with reporters and camera crews surrounding and focusing on who she once was.

"This is why I will never marry and have babies. No one should have to be hounded and followed with flashes going off in your face and people shouting your name. Especially innocents."

"Don't you think they've moved on to the next big story?"

"For now. At any time I could resurface on their radar. That's why I changed my name. I'm trying to live my life without being found. Without harming someone innocent with the shame of my life."

Kyle glanced over at her and she saw the sympathy in his eyes. "Tempe, you have a lot to be proud about. You're obviously a good vet. An intelligent woman who has gone through an inferno and came out whole on the other side. You're a survivor."

The words brought tears to her eyes. No one ever said anything kind to her since her mother's death, which caused her chest to tighten. Reaching over, he laid his hand on hers and squeezed, as warmth rushed through her at his touch.

CHAPTER 11

*A*fter she spilled her guts to Kyle about her background, getting to work on the animal was satisfying. It took her mind off her horrible past and back in the present, where another cow was ill.

And constipation wasn't her diagnosis. The heifer showed the same signs as Cody's cow. The rancher hovered nearby as she took blood samples. Another possible case. Another chance of a spreading epidemic.

"What bull inseminated her," she asked Joe knowing she'd aborted a calf.

"Old man Smith's prized bull broke down my fence. At the time, I thought the price for repairs was cheaper than the use of his semen."

Two cows, one bull, how many others had he infected?

"We'll get this off to the lab today. Hopefully they can let us know what the problem is," she said, trying to reassure the man, certain he had no idea of the repercussions. "Please keep her separate from all of your animals. This is just a precaution, kind of like when your kids have the measles. If she has a disease, we don't want it to spread."

Kyle gave the rancher a serious, concerned doctorly stare. "Joe, you don't want any other cattle to come down sick. When you see that bull - send him home with a raging hard on."

Tempe looked at Kyle, wondering if he had to be so graphic. Yet Joe laughed and she knew the vet had connected on a man's level. Men were so strange.

"You want to check her uterus or do you want me?" she asked.

Standing behind her, he grinned as the two men stood watching her work. "Go right ahead. The pleasure is all yours."

"Okay," she said, the cow securely in the squeeze chute where she couldn't kick Tempe. Lifting her tail, she shoved her hand in her private area only to hear the cow bawl her displeasure. With Tempe's hand inside the cow's uterus, she chose that moment to let loose and go to the bathroom.

Cow dung splat on her shirt, her pants and dripped down to her shoes. The odor, bad enough to make her nauseous and she almost lost her lunch right there. Even worse, the sound of laughter erupting.

Like she learned in school, she blotted our their snickers and continued with her examination. After several minutes of their laughter, she turned sideways to give the two a look that clearly expressed her annoyance, just as the heifer let go again. This time the excrement went flying to land on Kyle.

Now, they were both splattered. Her brows lifted and she shook her head as she stared at him. "Welcome to the party."

"Arrgh," he said disgusted. "What have you been feeding her Joe?"

The client was laughing. "Now you've gotten a taste of my world. Some damn cow poops on me at least once a day. My cows eat good old pasture grass. Texas best just landed on your chest."

To finish the exam, she pulled her hand out of the cow while the animal tried to poop again. Thank goodness, she was done. Finished examining her, she yanked the dirty gloves from her fingers, trying to keep from touching the outer portion. The joys of being a veterinarian.

Brucellosis was highly contagious to animals and people. Soap and water were needed, now.

"Whatever is wrong with her is certainly not intestinal. Now, we have to wait for the results of the tests," Tempe said glancing around. "Is there an outside place where I can wash up?"

The results would only confirm what Tempe suspected. Another case of Brucellosis. Another animal they would have to put down. Now they had two cases just waiting on confirmation.

"There's a water faucet, you can use on the other side of the barn," Joe told her. "I've got to run to the house for a moment, but you guys can clean up, so you don't go home smelling like roses."

Roses? Whoever thought that feces and flowers had a sweet aroma needed their olfactory organ examined.

"Thanks, I think I'll go with Dr. Tangier and rinse off as well, before we crawl back in my truck."

"You'll call me when you know something?"

"Yes, sir," Tempe said, tossing her soiled gloves in a plastic trash sack, she carried for that purpose. "Soon as the lab contacts me, we'll talk more. Let me know if her condition changes or worsens."

"Will do. Go get cleaned up. Both of you smell pretty bad," the rancher said as he walked away.

Cow crap, a hazard of the job that she disliked immensely. The stench unbearable as she hurried to the pump house wishing she had a change of clothes.

"Why is it that most cows use their poop as a defense mechanism?" Kyle asked as they reached the water hose. There were two water hoses hooked to the faucet, so they could each have one.

"Poor cow, if someone was sticking their hand in your privates and you couldn't kick or move, what other option do you have?"

With a frown Kyle ran the water over his hands, then he pulled his shirt from his pants and yanked it off.

"Are you going to rinse your shirt off right here?"

"Why not? It's better than stinking all the way back into town."

Carefully, she tugged her polo shirt over her head, mindful not to get any of the stinky mess in her hair. In the pasture, standing there in her bra, rinsing her shirt feeling his eyes on her a shiver scurried up her spine. "Eyes up, Doctor Lawrence."

He chuckled. "But the view is exceptional. Besides, they're in plain sight."

The look she gave him warned him away. After learning about her, she was surprised he hadn't run. "Let's remember the first time I saw you. Only a cowboy hat kept me from getting a glimpse of the full monty."

A grin crossed his face. "A man's gotta do what a man's gotta do."

Grinning, she squirted water at him, hitting him in the face.

"What the hell?"

"A woman's gotta do what a woman's gotta do."

Water gushed out of his hose and he placed his thumb over the metal opening, spraying water wide as he pointed it in her direction. Ice water splashed her, splattering her jeans.

"Not the pants," she said. "Or the boots."

"How about the breasts," he said grinning.

Taking her hose, she rushed at him, getting sprayed with water as he backed away from her. Relentless she went after him, slamming into his chest as the two of them went slipping on the damp grass and mud. Losing his footing, she felt herself falling. Down they went together, with her landing on top of him, the water gurgling between them, soaking the remaining clothes they wore.

Cold water soaked them, running into her underwear and she threw the hose away. Sprawled on him gazing into his brown eyes, she watched as they darkened. Wearing only her sports bra, his naked muscled chest against her breasts. What was she doing, laying out in the open half naked? With only a strip of clothing between them. She started to rise, but hesitated one second too long.

Stretched against him, she could feel his manhood hardening beneath her. "Is that a gun in your pocket?" she said in a whispery voice she didn't recognize.

"No, that's what you do to me," he said.

His tongue swiped across his mouth, his eyes locked on her. Why wasn't he running from her? The daughter of America's biggest swindler? Yet, she didn't want him to. The memory of their last kiss filled her and she longed to experience the caress of his lips against her own. To see if she would react to his kiss the same or had it only been that one time?

As if he read her mind, in answer to her question, his lips covered hers. Rolling her to her back, pressing into her, his legs firm and hard, his chest wet and warm and so thrilling.

The feel of his hands gripping her head, holding her mouth in place as he ravished her lips, plundering and taking what he wanted left her shivering. Never having been kissed like this before, she moaned deep in her throat, she didn't want this to end. Pulse pounding in her ears, her blood rushing through her, heating her body in areas never aroused before, Tempe clung to Kyle.

"Hey, Doc," Joe called.

Breaking apart, Kyle jumped to his feet and pulled her with him.

Quickly, she snatched on her wet polo over her head. What just happened?

Never before had she kissed a man until lust like a river flowed through her. Never before had she kissed a man until all she could think about was shedding her own clothes.

CHAPTER 12

*O*n Friday night, Kyle stared around at the Valentino's bar. Tempe stood at his side, watching as Meghan blew her candles out, celebrating her birthday. Country and western music blasted from the speakers and he wondered what his friends would think if they knew Scott Gaston's daughter was here in their midst.

She'd shocked him. Slowly, as the days went by, the realization of what she must have endured crept into his consciousness and overwhelmed him. No, she didn't want pity, but still the thought of his parents being involved in some kind of scandal that could have devastated their family would be heartbreaking. It was bad enough his father died so young and his mother soon after.

To this day, he still wanted to go running into the house, calling out for his mom and dad, telling them what had happened at school that day. But they were gone and life went on.

At Meghan's party he was standing here uncertainty thundering through him. Between Tempe's revelations and the stress of yet another sick heifer, he felt like his world was spinning out of control. They were still waiting on test results. Desperately, he needed to have fun.

"Come on Tempe, dance with me. You do know how to country and western dance, don't you?"

"Well, I can do a mean salsa."

"With peppers or without?"

Shaking her head at him, she said, "You are a goofball."

"Keeps life interesting. Why don't you salsa, and I'll do the two step."

The gravity of what she experienced and how she came out a winner stunned him. All evening he was reminded of the strength of this woman. At twenty-one he'd been busy working hard in school, getting his education, while his brother took care of the ranch.

Smiling at him she took his hand as he led her out on to the floor. Gracefully she fell into step with him.

The feel of her soft womanly curves pressed against him, the smell of her filling his lungs. Alone she buried her mother, changed her name and graduated college with a GPA high enough to get a scholarship into a veterinary program.

"The doctor can dance," he said twirling her.

"I never said I couldn't. All I said is I can salsa. Remember, my background. All society children take dance lessons. Don't want to make daddy look bad at an elegant ball."

Cringing inside, he couldn't imagine the life ripped from her. Even contemplating where she came from took some getting used to.

His eyes met hers in the darkened room and he didn't know how to handle the emotions roaring through him. So he did what he always did, he made a joke trying to alleviate his unease. "What a woman. She salsa's, two-steps, delivers puppies, and examines a cow's uterus. You're just an all around sexy girl."

"Okay, charm boy, turn it down a notch. The women in this

bar are looking at you like you're a tasty meal and they're starving. Somehow I gather you've been here before."

What could he say, he wasn't really a playboy, but like to come dancing at Valentino's and had been here enough times to have danced with quite a few of these women and taken several out.

"Let's say there never has been just any woman. I've dated, but becoming a vet consumed me from the time I entered college until I received my degree. Then I worked with another doctor in the city, until I came back to buy the old Doc out here in Cupid. So romance has not been a full time occupation for me."

"And now?"

With a quick glance around at the women standing on the edge of the floor. "Am I wrong to want a woman who is my equal?"

The words caused him to gaze at Tempe. The doctor was his equal in every sense of the word, she was smart, intelligent and would challenge him to be a better man, a better veterinarian. But she had drawbacks. Big ones, like, she was Scott Gaston's daughter. A vet from the USDA. Not no, but hell no.

Yet, cradled in his arms, she seemed so right, like she belonged beside him.Working together, they made a great team and was so laid back, easy going. Tempting lips beckoned him and glancing at her mouth as the blood rushed to his groin leaving him hard.

The music changed and he pulled her closer, feeling her body crushed against his own, her breasts rubbing on his chest, causing his blood to pump through his heart at a rapid speed.

There was no question what his friends were thinking. No way would you ever convince him Tempe came into in his life because of that statue. That had nothing to do with why she was here. In fact, he sent the original lab samples to the USDA.

"No, it's not wrong to want an equal," Tempe responded, her emerald eyes darkening as she stared at him. "If I were able to marry, an equal is exactly what I would want."

The memory of her kiss, the two of them rolling around on the ground like a couple of pigs in heat came back to him. Leaning in, he smelled the sweetness of her scent.

That day at the ranchers had been an exciting afternoon of working together. When the water fight ended with a kiss he'd wanted to bring her home and finish what they'd started. Instead, they had gone back to the clinic and after they cleaned up, gone out to dinner.

Today, they had waited all day for the test results, only to be disappointed. The tension of the day stretched between them like a tight wire connecting them. Only he wasn't certain it was just the results of the tests. Since that hot kiss, all he could think about was her in his bed. And he wanted her there now.

Knowing he was being forward, but unable to stop himself, he placed his hands on her buttocks and pressed her against him, letting her see what she did to him. No longer would he hide the way this woman tempted him. Even in college, no one ever enticed him the way Tempe had his blood heating.

For a second her green eyes went wide and then she tilted her head at him. "That gun of yours is cocked and loaded.""

The music stopped and they stood there a moment, staring. Somehow they had reached a crossroads. The blaze in her eyes shimmered in the light, a question in the gorgeous circles that he had the answer to. Yes, oh yes.

"We've made our appearance here, told her happy birthday. Maybe it's time to go home."

"Yes," she said, her voice breathless. "I'm ready."

"We're not going to say goodbye, let's go."

"Want to race?" she asked, her eyes large in the darkness.

There was so much he liked about this girl, that he had to keep reminding himself that she was the enemy. The agent from the USDA, sent to put down cows. Yet, she was so much more.

"I'll beat you out the door."

"Already halfway there," she said running.

He sprinted after her, certain that Dr. Tempe Tangier, daughter of a famous criminal would be in his bed tonight.

CHAPTER 13

*a*s they pulled up in the drive of the clinic, Tempe suddenly became nervous. On the dance floor, she'd been emboldened by the music, the crowd, the confidence she felt as a woman. But now, she wasn't certain coming back here, alone with Kyle, with this growing attraction between them was such a good idea.

Getting out of the car, they silently walked up to the front door. Had it only been four days ago, she sat in her car watching a naked man trying to break into the clinic?

And now as he opened the door and they walked inside the building, she swallowed nervously. What would they do now? There were still so many things Kyle didn't know about her.

Closing and locking the door behind him, Kyle turned to her, his earthy eyes gazing at her hungrily.

With a growl, Kyle lifted her into his arms, and toted her up the stairs. Shock rippled along her spine and she gasped. "What are you doing?"

"What I wanted to do days ago."

Heat filled her and she stared at him as he carried her through the door, kicking it closed with his foot. Did he understand they could never be together? Why would any man want to join with her and the shadow that clung to her.

Carrying her through the house, he took her into the bedroom, where he let her feet slide to the floor. Keeping her body tightly against his, she savored every hard inch of him, from his muscled ABS all the way to his rocklike thighs.

Though still clothed, the feel of his body--solid like stone, only warm and flexible--slid against her, igniting a fire in her womanly parts in response to the touch of his rigid male member.

"Do you want me?" he asked, his mouth close to her ear, his tongue tracing the lobe and running along her neck. "We're both in the moment people. Do you want to quench this heat between us?"

Her lungs seized and she moaned, giving him access to her shoulder, loving the ripples of slithering fieriness that shimmered through her.

"Yes, oh yes. I want you," she whispered, knowing she had waited for years for this moment.

CHAPTER 14

*L*ike a starving man, his lips covered her own, claiming her, branding her, demanding a response. Whimpering, she sagged against him, overwhelmed with the passion raging inside her. Her body was warming, heating to a level never before experienced. With a tug, he pulled her shirt over her head, his hands reaching for the waistband of her clothing.

Placing her hand on his chest, gasping for breath, she broke the kiss. "Wait."

Leaning down, she slipped her shoes off her feet. Then pushed him down on the bed. While there, she yanked off his cowboy boots and socks. Removing his shirt, he tossed it onto the floor and began to work on the belt at his waist.

Shucking her jeans, she reached up and unsnapped the hooks on her bra and let the garment fall. As he removed his pants, she ditched her panties and then drank in the sight of him.

What am I doing? But she pushed the rational thought aside and admired the beauty of his muscular body.

A lean, muscled body, his skin an even tone of brown, the cowboy had her breath stuttering. His manhood stood erect and a quiver went through her.

Life had been difficult, men scarce and while it seemed impossible, she waited never having the opportunity besides a quick fling in a bar. Not the way she dreamed of losing her virginity.

Gasping at the strength that exuded from him, she crawled onto the bed beside him. He grasped her arm and pulled her on top and she reveled in the touch of his velvety smooth skin over rigid muscles.

"We fit together, well," he said softly in her ear. "Your breasts crushed against my chest, your womanly pelvis smashed against me, make me want to take you hard and fast. Oh, Tempe, you've been a temptation since that very first night."

Kyle's words were like an inferno to her ears, causing her to cling to him as his mouth once again covered hers. Flipping her onto her back, his lips trailed down her chest, his hands gripping her own, holding them down on either side of her as he descended trailing kisses to her nipples.

At the caress of his mouth, she cried out as he drew the hardened kernel between his lips, suckling, carrying ripples of need centering in her middle. What was this feeling she never experienced before. Sure the textbooks had explained the sex act many times over, but she never participated in the act before tonight. And she was grateful Kyle was her first.

"Kyle," she sighed and he moved to the other breast, swirling his tongue around, lightly nipping her with his teeth.

"Oh," she moaned as her body came alive beneath his heated caresses.

When she thought she could experience nothing more, his fingers parted her legs and delved into her center. With a guttural sound of satisfaction at the moisture he found there, he teased her with his fingertips as she ached for something more.

With gentle strokes, she gasped. "Kyle."

"You're so tight," he whispered, his voice deep and throaty.

The idea crossed her mind that maybe she should tell him, but at this moment, she really didn't care. There was no time for explanations. Only the brush of his fingers, the skim of his caress, the deepening of his gaze were all that mattered.

Reaching over, he opened a drawer and pulled out a package. In a matter of moments, he rolled the latex down over his member.

Rising over her, he spread her open with his muscular thighs, his powerful tool advancing against the opening that eagerly wanted him. Staring into the gleam of his eyes, she watched as with a groan, he thrust, pressing until he filled her. The sting of pain, nothing compared to the flames pulsing through her.

"What the hell," he said with a gasp. "You're a virgin."

"Please, don't stop," she cried.

They were joined as one, and passion drove every question from her as he plunged into her time and again, climbing, reaching for something she'd never experienced. With every thrust, she felt as if his name was being scrolled across her heart. With every stroke, he made her his own. With every kiss, she became his.

Seeking to understand, she stared into his eyes, and her world started to unravel. Like the universe was exploding as every cell strove toward the brilliant light that flashed through her, sending shock waves rattling like a tidal wave washing her ashore.

In a husky voice, she heard Kyle call her name as his body shattered around her, clinging to her like two lost souls adhered by a mere thread to the earth.

Slumping over her he rolled to her side, cradling her body against him. Both breathed like a race horse after a race, their chests aching for more air. In silence, she lay beside him, unwinding as the tingles disappeared, leaving a behind a sense of bliss.

Running her fingertips along the arm that cradled her, tears pricked her eyes. What the hell had she done? She gave herself to a man, told him of her past, left herself vulnerable to hurt and manipulation. Was she crazy? The lawyer warned her and in a moment of passion, she'd broken every rule he gave her.

CHAPTER 15

*A*fterwards Kyle, gazed at her. Why hadn't she told him she was a virgin? Would it have made a difference?

"Okay, I'm scared. Most women don't make it past the first semester of college without losing their virginity. Yet here you are."

"In college, I was still Tempe Gaston. My father and his associates were all on trial, while I attended school. Only because of the inheritance I acquired from my mother, could I afford to go. It wasn't easy. During the court case, I learned to be creative to walk across campus without reporters following me. But a party life?"

A sarcastic giggle escaped from her lips. "No sorority would consider me. Who would want to date a girl whose parents probably lost money because of her father? Quickly, I became the social outcast. Sometimes ridiculed. Always the object of pranks."

Kyle remembered his years in college, the ones where he had been partying and learning and figuring out how to be an adult. A young woman having to deal with a family crisis, so public she couldn't go anywhere without reporters trailing her every move would be difficult. Not to mention, the kids in school hating you. Inside his stomach clenched, hurting for her.

"After my mother killed herself, the lawyer convinced me to change my name. Before I entered the veterinary program at Colorado State University - halfway across the continent away from my poisonous family, I changed my name.

Funny, he thought about going to that school, but chose Texas A&M instead. The urge to her happiness overcame him and he held her tight. After all, she went through, she deserved someone to care for her and make her happy. Right now, he intended to be that man.

A smile crossed her face. "Even then I feared graduating at the head of my class afraid someone would see my picture and recognize me. So I graduated number eleven. Just below the top ten, not to draw attention."

"How did you go to work for the USDA?"

A heavy sigh came from her and he knew talking about all this stuff must be painful for her. "Actually, they recruited me. The salary is nice and I decided the job would help me reach my goal quicker."

The thought of trying to get your education while your life is played out on national television must have been horrifying. Bullies were like a bad traffic day in Dallas, coming at you from all directions.

"Have you tried to get a loan and start a practice?" he asked.

Shaking her head, she snorted. "The banks are always excited to talk to me, until they learn my true identity. Then they run. Tempe Gaston is connected to the man who cost them millions and though I'm innocent, no one is willing to take a chance on me."

With startling clarity he realized this would follow her the rest of her life. No wonder she said she couldn't drag anyone into her screwed up life. One smart, investigative reporter could hunt her down and make her existence hell.

"Tempe Tanzier doesn't have enough credit to obtain a loan to open her own hospital. So here I am, working, saving, building a large down payment for a bank to lend me enough money to get me started."

A pang of sympathy went through Kyle, causing his chest to tighten. He'd been fortunate. The inheritance he received bought the old vet's clinic.

For years Kyle recognized he was blessed. Not only had his parents left each one of their children a lump sum, but also shares in the family ranch. Jim was the CEO and main owner, but the others still had a stake in the operation.

Watching the graduates of his class, struggle he was grateful to his parents forethought and consideration .

"How long have you been with them?"

"A year.," she said, snuggling up against his body. "I'll probably be with them at least one more."

Quietly, he sat and held her again thinking back to what started this conversation. Being her first was an honor that she'd chosen him, but he still had questions that needed answered.

"You've waited all this time to give yourself to a man. Why me and why now?"

With her back to his chest, he couldn't see her expressions and needed to see her face. He rolled her over, keeping her in his arms.

"Come on, I'm twenty-six. No one believes you're a virgin. You feel like you're missing out on life. Teenagers are doing what I had never experienced. This just seemed like the right time."

Rolling over on top of her nude body, loving the way she felt beneath him, Kyle stared into her emerald eyes, warmth flowing between them. "So I'm nobody special."

With a laugh, she glanced into his eyes. "Oh, you're special all right. You're the first man I've considered since I left school. There, I was too frightened to let the walls down."

Gripping her hands in his, he raised himself up and shoved

into her again. "If your walls are down, then maybe its time for the conquerer to take advantage."

"Conquerer?" she said, her body moving in time with his.

"Oh yes, me," he said as his mouth covered hers.

CHAPTER 16

*T*empe awoke the next morning to the sounds of the busy clinic downstairs. A quick glance at the clock and she sat straight up, amazed at how late she slept. An early riser, she couldn't believe the time was almost nine. Jumping out of bed, her feet barely reached the ground when her phone started ringing.

She ran across the bedroom to where her purse lay and grabbed her cell.

"Doctor Tangier," she said.

"This is Doctor Everest."

"Good morning, John how are you?"

Immediately, she knew what this meant. The results of the tests were in. This was the call she'd been waiting for to learn the fate of that poor animal, though her gut instinct had already made the diagnosis.

The man ignored her pleasantries, which was normal for him. A no nonsense doctor he never minced words.

"You've got a problem. Brucellosis is confirmed. The cow must be put down and the herd quarantined."

A sigh slipped out. It was never easy putting an animal down unless they suffered and even then it was difficult. Years ago she learned never to become attached to her patients, but still you cared about them. Probably more so because they depended on you.

"The entire herd?" she asked. "I'm almost certain I know how this happened and who is patient zero. My plan is to do blood work on the herd so we find all contaminated cattle."

Knowing that would be her next step and then on to see the owner of the bull. There would be a couple of very unhappy ranch owners. Bulls could be worth hundreds of thousands of dollars and generate thousands of dollars of income. Income that ranchers lived on.

"What about the herd?" Doctor Everest asked. "Are any of the other cattle ill? Aborting the fetus?"

Cody Graham seemed honest with her, but she would need to ask him specific questions.

"Not that I'm aware. The local vet, Dr. Lawrence, separated the animal as soon as he suspected the disease."

"Whole herds have been wiped out because of this infection. The best interest for the rancher would be to test the herd. Though costly."

But at the risk of losing all of his cattle, it might be wise. "Let me assess the situation and I'll get back to you."

"Doctor Tangier don't let anyone talk you into shortcuts. If this grows any larger, the USDA team will swoop down on us and make your investigation more burdensome."

A trickle of fear spiraled up her spine. Losing a herd would devastate any rancher. And she didn't want, the leader of the team from the USDA here to answer to. The epidemics group, were more of a clean-up crew who slaughtered infected animals and quarantined areas. Kyle needed to be warned.

"As soon as I have more definitive information, I'll be in touch. At that point we can decide our next course of action," she said, wishing she wasn't standing here with nothing but a sheet wrapped around her. They weren't using FaceTime, but still she'd feel more professional in her working clothes.

"Good luck. Let me know if you need any help," the older veterinarian said.

"Yes," she said. It was her first really serious contagious outbreak, but she could handle the outcome.

Hitting the end call button, she glanced around the room. Last night had been wonderful. Though she had nothing to compare to, being with Kyle made her think of things she gave up years ago. Things like a husband and family, but in the light of day, the realization those dreams were delusions for a woman like her left her stomach aching.

Fun loving Kyle, was kind and they shared so many common interests. If only her life was different.

How would Kyle take the news, especially since his future brother-in-law Cody's heifer would be the first animal put down.

Today the reality of why she was here came from a phone call like a slam to her chest.Time to return to work. Time to do her job.

Not a great day after a wonderful night.

CHAPTER 17

$\mathcal{C}$ody Graham was not happy and Tempe could understand his reaction. "I'm sorry, I realize why you're upset. But I need to know how she was inseminated and the name of the bull."

"Ed Smith's bull. It happened by accident. Didn't I tell you this once already?" he sai, his voice rising.

"Yes, you did," she said not wanting to say she just wanted to verify his story remained the same. "What about your other cattle? This heifer has been isolated away from the others, but do you have any other cows who aborted their babies?"

"No, she's the only one."

"When I pulled the records it shows she's been vaccinated."

"When I bought her at an auction, I assumed all the shots were taken care of," he said shaking his head. "That day, I purchased several cattle."

Kyle stood off to the side, his arms crossed, his feet firmly planted on the ground, like he was taking a stand. The lover from last night was gone, replaced by the protective friend and doctor.

Why had she gotten involved with the people in the small

town? Now she would have to do her job, possibly hurting the friends she made, in the process.

"Vaccination is not a guarantee the animal will not come down with the infection. It makes her chances less of becoming ill. Unfortunately, since the disease is highly contagious and spread through fluids, I'm going to have to quarantine your herd. They are not to be sold or moved until we're certain this infection is limited to right here and this cow."

Cody's face turned red. "What the hell? Roundup is coming up and then we decide how many head to send to market."

"Until I'm convinced your cows are clean, those cattle go nowhere."

As she prepared the injection that would end the poor cow's life, she stopped and glanced at him. "Look, this could ruin most ranchers. I'll do my best to aid you in any way I can, but we've got to test every one of your cattle. It's imperative we make certain none of your other cattle are infected."

"How much is this going to cost me?"

"We'll work out the details later. Government subsidies can help pay for this, but we'll only be putting down the infected cattle."

Kyle stepped up beside his friend and put his hand on his shoulder. "Don't worry, I've got your back. If you need some help, I'm here. Jim and Drew will help as well. You're family."

Tempe sighed as warmth cascaded through her. Unlike herself, at least Cody had Kyle and his brothers.

"Thank you for the offer, but I don't want to be beholding to anyone," he said.

Piercing the cow she noticed the way, Kyle hung back, a tightness on his expression, his jaw clenched. In a matter of minutes, the animal took her last breath and sadness overcame Tempe. Always, she mourned a death.

Standing up the two men slid the deceased heifer onto a trailer, where they would haul the carcass to an incinerator.

A frown on his face, Cody stared. "So now what? You've quarantined my herd. Killed my sick cow. Should I expect more death and destruction?"

This wasn't her fault, but the bearer of the bad news always took the most blowback. And in the past year, she'd come to accept that it was just a continuation of how people treated her after her father's heist became public knowledge.

"In the morning, I will speak to Mr. Smith and then I'll be out here to begin testing the herd. The sooner we do this, the sooner we'll know the size of this outbreak."

Packing up her supplies, took only a few moments. "This disease could wipe out everyone's herd, not just yours."

A few minutes later, Kyle helped her up in the truck.

As they drove off the property, he spun the tires. "Whoa, please remember you're pulling a trailer with a dead cow in the back."

"Sorry," he said curtly.

The man was hurting for his friend, he was angry, but her hands were tied. The rules and regulations of the USDA required that cow be put down. There was no cure. There was no way to stop the spread other than to kill the animals who caught the dreaded sexually transmitted disease.

Yet, that didn't make her feel any better concerning Kyle or even his friend Cody.

Kyle hit his hand against the steering wheel. "In this modern day with inspections, rules and regulations regarding our food source, how does this happen? We spent two weeks learning about Brucellosis in my infectious disease class. Why my best friend?"

She hated to break it to him, but disease didn't care who it affected.

"Isn't there any other way to save his herd?"

"We're going to test each animal. Soon we'll know for certain what we're dealing with. In the meantime, I'll meet with Mr. Smith."

Glancing over at her, he shook his head. "If that bull tests positive, he'll be furious."

Watching the landscape glide by the window, she remembered the act of friendship she witnessed between Cody and Kyle. That offer of help to a friend, had been touching. The memory of her childhood friends, the girls she hung with until the press broke the story about her father, the ones who ditched her faster than a racing car.

Moving half a continent away, she no longer endured their painful snubs. Sometimes she missed the friendships, the lunches, the parties, the hanging together.

In this world, Tempe had no one.

CHAPTER 18

*S*ometimes the unfairness of life, the disregard for animals lives, the disease, the mistreatment overcame Kyle and he wanted to scream at the heavens, why? Why did this happen to Cody or to any rancher for that matter? It wasn't that he didn't know what he was getting into when he went to school, he longed for the opportunity to work with animals.

Still, not every day was sunshine and puppy kisses. And today was one of those days when he questioned why hadn't he become a banker or a lawyer like his brother. Why not deal with something a little less painful.

The clinic was closed by the time they returned, his staff had all gone home. At the door, they were greeted by the sound of barking dogs.

Together they walked up the stairs to his quarters and he went straight to the refrigerator and grabbed himself a beer.

A chance to dull the misery inside him. The chance not to hurt so much at the knowledge he delivered the trouble on his friend, his brother. After all, he sent in the sample that brought the USDA to the doorstep.

Knowing the risks Brucellosis could bring, he did what he

thought was right, hoping his suspicions were not correct. Only to harm his best friend, someone he loved.

"Want a beer?" he asked, closing the fridge.

"Sure," she said and he handed her one.

Walking out to the patio she slumped down on the swing, staring out at the little town. Slowly she sipped the alcohol, not saying anything.

As he sank down beside her, he tried to push the feelings away, but anger surged through him. The outcome was so unfair and he felt the urge to make her feel his pain. "You enjoy putting down animals?"

Turning on the bench to face him, her eyes flashed a glare that should have warned him. For a moment, he feared she would hit him over the head with the beer bottle. And he knew his words had been a low blow, but he seethed with the outrage of it all.

"Oh yeah, I went to school to learn how to torture animals. My favorite part of the day is killing an animal who is ill, " she said, her voice dripping with sarcasm. Her body stiff with frustration. "How about you? Is that why you immediately came in and went to the refrigerator for alcohol?"

Since they left Cody's he wanted to fight, to argue with Tempe. Damn, but he hated euthanizing an animal, he hated dealing with this terrible infection and he hated she seemed so cool on the outside. Why couldn't he respond with that same logical preciseness?

"This is my future brother-in-law. The man who is marrying my sister. The people in this town are my friends and family. I don't want them to suffer because of this situation."

"I don't want the animals to suffer."

"You just seem to enjoy your job a little too much," he said taking a swig of beer.

For about thirty seconds, a deathly silence hung in the air between them and then like a lioness she attacked.

"Look charm boy, I hate this damn job. The rules, the regulations and all the sanctimonious good ole boys, I work with on a daily basis. My life plan was to be a vet. To open up my own hospital and take care of animals, not travel from ranch to ranch, telling the owner he's got a problem. Or that his inspections came back negative."

Her chest rose as she took a deep breath and pulled back her shoulders. Like a machine gun she fired shots at him.

"Being the watch dog for the government is not a fun job. But neither is being the daughter of a man who stole millions. Do you know what it's like to witness an army of people come into your house and catalog all your worldly possessions. To see the brand new Porsche given to you for high school graduation impounded. To stand by and see your mother cry helplessly as her antiques are taken for auction? I'm glad you have family and friends you cherish, I don't have a clue what that feels like."

Standing, she polished off the rest of her beer.

"Don't ever think I enjoy this job. This is not who I want to be."

In a quick jerky move, she turned and walked into the house and he heard the door slam close.

Sitting there alone, he suffered even more than he had when they arrived home. He'd been a dick. An absolute ass to a woman he realized he cared about. A woman he grew fonder of each day. A smart, intelligent doctor whom the world had kicked in the teeth.

Just now, he verbally bullied her, but this time Dr. Tangier was learning to kick back. She certainly put him in his place and left him aching with the realization how he acted like a heel.

Last night they'd shared such a closeness and intimacy, tonight instead of sharing the anguish they both were hurting from, he tried to turn her into the bad guy and make her ache with guilt. Only this time she stood her ground and let him learn what a jerk he was.

Maybe he was crazy, but the way she put him in his place, made him respect her even more.

CHAPTER 19

*T*empe squared off against the rancher. This morning she'd risen early and left without saying a word to Kyle. After last night's comments, she needed some distance. Anyone who thought working for the USDA was enjoyable and rewarding should be forced to see a specialist in mental health.

The paperwork was enough to send you to an asylum. Not to mention the gracious owners who screamed, yelled and cursed her when she gave them the bad news. People were suspicious of anyone who showed up from the government, right or wrong.

"You're crazy as a loon if you think I'm letting you put down my prized bull. He's the biggest money maker I've got."

"Has he recently been tested for Brucellosis?"

"He don't need testing. My bull has no venereal disease."

Silently she regarded the man. "Did your bull break down a fence between you and Cody Graham? Between you and Joe McBowen?"

The man sighed. "Yeah, so what if he did."

"Yesterday I euthanized a heifer over at Mr. Graham's and this afternoon I'll be speaking to Mr. McBowen about one of his cows."

"That don't mean they caught it from one of my cattle," he said.

"No it doesn't, but that mean looking cow is suspected of harboring a contagious disease. Now we can do this one of two ways. You can help me draw blood from him or I can call out my team and we can shut down your operation. Which is it going to be?"

Lifting his hat he ran his hand through his hair, all the while glaring at her like he contemplated murder. "And you'll put him down if you find Brucellosis?"

"There's no cure, it's highly infectious and sexually transmitted. I have no choice. This bull will be tagged - no one will want his sperm.

The man swore a string of words that made Tempe blush. Then he stopped and stared at her.

"You're a very smart woman to be doing this job. What if I gave you a ten thousand dollar shopping spree."

Her blood froze in her veins, not moving. To anyone else using that kind of cash for shopping would seem outlandish, but she remembered the trips to New York where money was no object. Tempe and her mother dropped thousands of dollars going from shop to shop. Spending cash like that in one day was easy and fun.

She'd known they were blessed, but had no idea what doing without wealth really meant. Never in her life had she worried about money. Now she lived like the rest of America, one paycheck at a time.

The offer was tempting just to relive old times, but unethical. Since her father's arrest, her sense of right and wrong was heightened. Yes, she was Scott Gaston's daughter, but that didn't mean she stole or took bribes.

Tempe Tangier would never cheat people or steal. After the Gaston empire crumbled, she made a vow to live above reproach by the law. She had to atone for the sins of her father.

Tilting her head, she looked at him sideways. "Now, I certainly hope that's not a bribe, because if it is, then I'm required to contact my supervisor. A team of investigators comes out and shuts your operations down while they do their job. The fine is quite high and there is even a jail term sentence involved."

The man's mouth thinned and he clinched his fists. "Of course I'm not bribing you. A pretty little thing like you would like some new clothes."

What woman wouldn't like new clothes, new shoes, even a new designer handbag. But that Tempe no longer existed, she'd been replaced and now went to big box department stores for everything.

"Oh I love me some new clothes, but not at the expense of doing my job," she said giving him her no nonsense don't mess with me look. "So what is it going to be?"

The man all but growled at her. "Take the damn sample. My hands will put him in the chute for you. This test better come back clean. That bull is worth a hundred thousand dollars."

"Mr. Smith, I hope for yours and the bulls sake, the results are negative."

"I'll get my kit," she said walking to her car.

Today, might have been a good time for Kyle to be with her, but the man overstepped his bounds last night and pushed her to her limit. No one accused her of wanting to put down animals. That just pissed her off.

CHAPTER 20

*K*yle missed Tempe today. This morning he awoke to an empty apartment and at first he feared she left for good. Opening the door, he had peeked into the room she slept in and seen her suitcases and sighed with relief.

Okay, so last night he overstepped his bounds and acted like a jerk. The events of the day pained him and he lashed out at the person he thought caused him agony. But Tempe shouldn't be blamed for what happened yesterday.

That would be like blaming the doctor who delivered the cancer diagnosis. The bearer of bad news, she shouldn't be held responsible for Cody's cow being put down.

Still, she'd been an easy target and afterwards he recognized he had been a real jackass.

After delivering puppies at his brother Jim's house, he'd returned back to the clinic, hoping she was there, but no Tempe.

Close to seven and she had yet to come in. Beginning to worry, he kept watch from the patio. He wanted her help with his plans for tonight. They both needed to laugh and release some stress. First he would have to eat some crow. Feathers and all, he was going to have to fall at the bottom of her feet and beg for mercy.

Sitting outside, he observed her parking her car at the back of the clinic. Turning the motor off, she stepped out and glanced up at him, her face drawn in the fading light. Like a horny teenage boy, eager for his first date he waved at her. Good grief, all day he watched for her, waiting on her to return.

Her auburn hair like a beacon glinting in the last bit of sunlight and he wanted to reach out and brush it back away from her face. Longed to kiss her full lips and hold her tight against his chest once again. No doubt about it, he screwed up last night.

A few minutes later, she came out onto the patio and sank down in a chair not far from him. Not on the swing next to him. She was distancing herself and that's not what he wanted.

"You're back late," he said.

"Busy day."

An awkward moment of silence hung between them and he couldn't wait any longer. Taking a deep breath, he released it slowly. He hated apologizing. Even when he was wrong, but he needed to say something.

"Look about last night." Running his hand through his hair, trying to calm his nerves, he licked his lips and stared at her.

"Sometimes when I'm hurting, I say things I shouldn't. No doctor enjoys putting down his patients. Animals are very special to us and you didn't enjoy euthanizing that heifer anymore than I did. Because I know what this disease could do to my friends and family, I'm scared. I apologize for the hurtful things I said to you, I was insensitive and mean."

Kyle felt like a huge lump of clay clogged his throat. It wasn't in his nature to be vicious and vindictive and yesterday he was both. Apologizing stung, but he'd been wrong.

With a tilt of her head, she gazed at him, her emerald eyes wide, her brows raised as if surprised. "Thank you. Apology accepted. Since school, I dread having to end an animal's life. I'm not God, yet I don't want them to suffer either."

Amazed, Kyle stared at her. Yes, he was certain most vets detested deciding who lived and who died, but she said it so eloquently.

"It's the same for me. There are so many things, I love about my job, but having to make the decision to say goodbye, is difficult. Even when you try not to become emotionally involved, there's a part of you that questions am I doing what's best for the animal?"

Nodding her head, she looked at him her eyes still wary. "Last night I knew you were upset, but then you touched on the wound I sometimes wonder will ever heal. That's when I had to leave."'

With a nervous swallow, he perceived Tempe was like a wounded animal and he had worked so hard to gain her trust, only to squander it on a stupid, couple of words. Now it would take time to recover.

At the realization of the pain he created for her, his chest tightened. "The moment the words left my mouth, I knew I'd said the wrong thing. It was too late and I couldn't pull them back."

Shaking her head, she stared at him. "What is it between the two of us? Maybe because we're both vets, but there is this attraction I can no longer deny. I've shared with you things I'm not supposed to talk about. That also means we have the ability to wound the other person really bad. Last night you hurt me."

Well, that certainly didn't make him feel any better. In fact, now he seemed like a bigger louse.

"You're right. The only thing I can say is I'm sorry."

With a sigh, she said, "Let's put this behind us."

Relief poured through him, leaving his knees weak. At the thought of her saying goodbye, he'd been anxious and scared.

Now, their first big fight was behind them, but still that didn't warrant there was anything to the Cupid statue. Or that they were meant to be together. No matter what, he just wasn't ready for her to go.

"Great idea."

"In fact, I'll tell you about my day. The man who owns the bull we suspect started this fiasco that brought me to town, I went to see him."

"Please tell me you didn't go out there alone. That man can be a mean SOB."

A chuckle escaped from her. "Oh yeah, you wouldn't believe the stunt he pulled. That crazy old fool tried to bribe me."

Laughing, he pictured poor Ed Smith not understanding that just because Tempe was a woman, he could persuade her to break the law. The man obviously didn't realize she was a strict by the book kind of girl. Suddenly he thought about her father and considered the reason for her being so rules focused.

Could part of the justification for her being so precise be her father's lawlessness? Could she be trying to convince herself, she was not like him?

"The man tried to give me a ten thousand dollar shopping trip," she giggled almost hysterically. "What he doesn't under-stand is me and my mother use to drop thousands in a store. Mother and I would go shopping and come back with a whole new wardrobe."

A heavy sigh filled the night. "We were so extravagant. I miss not having money worries, but no one buys me off. No one," she said determination filling her voice. "Yes, I'm my father's daugh-ter, but that doesn't mean I'm like him."

Kyle's heart ached at the agony, her father brought upon her. Without thinking he rose from his chair and walked over to her and pulled her up. If he could, he would soothe and take away her hurt, but that was impossible.

So instead he wrapped his arms around her and held her. Now was not the time to try to kiss her. He simply comforted her, knowing Tempe Tangier had every reason to feel saddened missing her old life.

CHAPTER 21

*K*yle was on edge waiting for a call confirming what he hoped his sister and future brother-in-law would do tonight.

The time for the payback was upon Cody, though he didn't know it yet.

The phone rang and he answered his cell. "What did you find out?"

Jim laughed. "Tonight is their three month anniversary and she's leaving work early for them to celebrate."

Kyle smiled into the receiver. "Oh, they'll be celebrating in style. Thanks Jim. I promise you big brother, I'm going to give them a night to remember."

The night he ran the Cupid dance, Cody had stolen their clothes. Tonight, if things went according to plan, he would receive his payback.

"Don't call me from jail or the hospital with a bullet wound," Jim warned. "We've both recovered from that night."

Kyle wanted to ask Jim about his love life, but decided if he did, that could lead to questions he wasn't prepared to answer.

"Oh, I won't," he promised. "I'm just going to steal their clothes."

"Call me when you're home safe and sound and tell me how it went."

Sometimes his brother was worse than a parent, always wanting to make certain they were all okay. But again, his mother made him promise to watch over them and Jim had taken good care of them all.

"Will do," Kyle said and hung up the phone.

Walking in the downstairs area of the clinic, he found Tempe going through one of his veterinary manuals. "I need your help," he said, grabbing her hands and pulling her to her feet.

"What?"

"You'll see. Come on," he said and started dragging her towards the door.

"Let me grab my purse," she said.

In his truck heading down the highway, she turned to him. "Is this an emergency?"

Not wanting to tell her, everything for fear she'd back out, but she needed to know most of the truth. Yet he feared that if she learned what they were doing, before they left, she would back out. Tempe was not exactly a prankster.

"No, this is revenge."

"Oh? Why would I want to participate?"

Already she was questioning her involvement. The woman needed to loosen up a little. This is what you did in a small town. Played pranks on one another. Especially your friends.

"Because the night I ran around the Cupid statue naked, Cody stole mine and Jim's clothes. That night you saw me in my birthday suit. Tonight, I seek revenge."

"Again, why would I want to participate?"

With a grin at her, he said, "Because you want to help me. I'm a charming man who needs your participation in order to pull this off."

"Keep talking," she said, watching him.

"You're beautiful, smart and intelligent and you'll do a great job helping me."

She started laughing. "How could any woman resist that? Make certain that we don't end up in handcuffs. The last thing I need is a law man checking into my past."

"Oh no, we'll be out on his private property. While he and my sister are sitting naked in the hot tub, we're going to steal their clothes and lock the house, so they have no way back in."

"How do you plan on doing that?"

"During the time they're engaged with each other - lips locked that sort of thing, I'm going to sneak out and pilfer their robes and shoes. Then I'm going to lock them out of the house without any clothes."

His biggest concern he hoped he didn't catch them in the act. That would be really embarrassing for them and for Kyle.

"You don't get even, you get ahead," she said.

"I don't think so. They're out in the country. Cody, left me high and dry in the town square without a stitch of clothes to put on."

Actually, they were at home and somehow Cody would find a way into the house. Unlike himself, who had to reach the clinic.

"You still had your hat," she responded, grinning at him.

"No, that was Cody's hat and he gave it to me after I covered my junk with it."

Shaking her head, she tilted it and gazed at him, sending a trickle of lust racing down his spine. "What do you want me to do?"

"Your job is to go in the house and lock it up, while I grab their robes and shoes. By the time we're done, they're going to be bare assed naked. A sight I don't want to see, so we're going to need to hurry back to the truck."

"Don't you think they'll have a spare key somewhere?"

This woman not only enticed him physically, but he liked the way her mind worked. An evil sounding chuckle echoed from his chest. "Already thought of that. Last week he showed me where the extra key was in the barn. Tonight, it goes missing."

"How will they get in?" she asked, concern in her voice.

Stretching over he patted her on the leg. "Guess he'll have to either break a window or call a locksmith. Not my problem," he said. "After all I had to run through the town square to Jim's truck and drive from there back to the clinic without clothes. I'm repaying the favor."

"What about hypothermia?"

Turning his vehicle down the road to their place he switched off the lights. A thrill of anticipation gripped his stomach. The last time he and Cody gave each other a payback, they'd been in high school.

"It gets a little chilly, but they'll be fine. Besides, his barn has a nice apartment near the hayloft."

She glanced over at him. "You boys certainly know how to stir up trouble."

A grin spread across his face. "That's right. This is what living in a small town is like."

When they came to the drive, he parked the truck and turned off the engine. "We walk from here."

"What if there are snakes crawling?"

A frown deepened the furrows between his brows. "Snakes? No way. They're afraid of my bite."

Stepping out of the truck, she shook her head. "Let's do this."

Sneaking down the driveway, first they went to the barn, where Kyle quickly found the key and put it in his pocket. Hurrying back to the house, the sound of laughter reached his ears and he knew the couple sat in the hot tub.

At the front door, he whispered in Tempe's ear. "Make certain you lock all the doors. Their robes should be hanging on hooks on the back of the privacy fence. I'll reach over, take their clothes and then we'll haul butt out of here."

If Cody caught them, he wouldn't press charges, because brothers didn't do that. This was all a little harmless fun or so he hoped.

"Be careful. This is craziness."

Grabbing her he gave her a quick kiss. "And it's fun."

They separated and he watched her open the front door of the house and walk in. Five minutes later, he made his way around to the back where the three quarters privacy fence shielded the hot tub from the road. Soaking in the relaxing tub, they could gaze on the pasture, but from the lane all you could see was the wooden partition.

Reaching over the top, he grabbed both robes at the same time. Just when he thought he'd gotten away, he heard his sister. "What happened to my robe? I left it hanging there?"

A trickle of alarm had him quietly slipping away, his heart pounding in his chest. If Tempe hadn't had time to lock the doors, they would be caught.

"Honey, you don't need your robe," Cody replied. "I'm sure it's still in the house."

"I didn't walk out here nude. Where is yours?"

Loud cursing erupted and Kyle started running. Cody knew.

He ran as fast as his two feet would carry him back to the front of the house, where Tempe was standing outside waiting. Thank goodness, Cody couldn't cut through the house.

Loaded down with their robes and shoes, he didn't care, he was feeling pretty successful.

"Come on," he said. "Run."

"Oh no, did they catch you?"

Charging down the drive together, Tempe laughed.

He chuckled. "No, but they realized something happened to their clothes."

Giggling, they hurried to the truck, threw the robes and shoes in the back and jumped in. Starting the engine, Kyle turned on the lights and spun out on the road.

Glancing up in the rearview mirror, Cody stood naked as the day he was born in the middle of his drive shaking his fist at him. A smile crossed his face as he kept on driving. Paybacks were hell.

"Don't look behind us, but we just got caught. Good, I wanted him to realize who locked him out. Now he knows."

Tempe grinned at him in the darkness, the light reflecting off her face. "So now has the debt been repaid?"

"Now, I don't owe him until he does something to us again."

"Never met, crazier," she said. "But I have to admit, that was kind of fun."

CHAPTER 22

*S*everal days later, after being forced to put down yet another heifer, Tempe made the decision to hold a town meeting to inform the local ranchers. Rumors were beginning to circulate and if the infection was spreading, she wanted to make the owners aware. Glancing around the packed room, filled with cowboys, she realized she was probably the most hated woman in the room. A trickle of uneasiness spiraled down her spine, like a warning.

The mayor stood in front of the crowd and called everyone to order. "Thanks for coming on such short notice. The USDA brought it to my attention that we've got a possible epidemic brewing in our community. An agent is here to explain what's going on. Please welcome Dr. Tempe Tangier."

With a splattering of applause, Tempe rose and walked to the podium. "My agency is probably not who you like to see, but we wanted to inform you why we're here. How you can help to stop the transmission of Brucellosis."

All the ranchers who were there knew the name of the disease and immediately the chatter amongst themselves started.

Her first response was to say something, but then she waited, knowing if she said anything, it would only make things worse.

With the news being divulged today, Kyle's family came to support him standing along the wall of the small room.

"Quiet," the mayor called.

"This is a venereal disease that cattle spread. Some of the symptoms are, spontaneous abortion, weak calves, stillborn, signs of contagion in the membranes and swollen testicles on bulls. Any animal acting abnormal, should be separated from the others or if you suspect, please contact me or Dr. Lawrence.."

"Yes, but won't you quarantine our herds if we do?" a man in the back yelled.

Of course she would stop the bovine from being sold, but that wasn't the end of the world. Losing your herd would be more devastating than holding the cows back until you determined they weren't spreading the contamination.

"Unfortunately, Brucellosis is highly contagious. Do you want it to infect your neighbor's animals? Do you want the USDA to shut down all purchases of cattle in this area?"

"That's the problem with the government, they're not looking out for the little rancher. I bet you've already tested an approved the big money making outfits. You're just trying to weed out the smaller ranchers."

Tempe sighed. Why did everyone believe the evil bureaucracy wanted to put them out of business. "Mr.?" she asked, wanting to know his name.

"David Jones of the Big J Ranch."

"Mr. Jones, I've been to three ranches. Before I go out, I have no idea how large a ranch or how many cows they own. In all three cases, they were not a commercial outfit, only your neighbors. So far two heifers have been put down and the owner's cattle quarantined until we run tests. Once completed, the quarantine will be lifted if there are no other signs of infection. I'm waiting on the test results of the other animal."

The memory of the reporters shouting questions to her like she was the enemy came back and she had to fight the impulse to run. To dodge their queries and race out the door. A shudder rippled through her, centering in her chest radiating pain from that terrible time.

She'd gotten signed releases from the two ranchers she had put down heifers. The bull...she glanced at his owner standing in the back of the crowded room. Less than twenty minutes ago, the test results came back and he was not going to be happy at the outcome.

The USDA and the disease gave her no choice. The animal was an infectious threat that could contaminate other ranchers' herds. Especially if he liked to tear through fences to get what he wanted.

The irritating man jumped up. "Tell us who you quarantined."

Taking a deep breath, she pushed down the urge to run. Didn't they understand the infection was the enemy, not her, she was trying to help. "That's not my place. If they choose to come forward that's their decision."

A rumble of dissatisfaction came from the men and she felt like they were a band of tribal men circling the fire preparing to sacrifice her to the volcano.

Cody stood. "One of them was my heifer. Now we're testing the herd."

"How did she become infected?" The man shouted at Cody.

Right now, Tempe didn't like the way this meeting was going and as soon as she could, she would end it. These men came here looking for the blood of a salaried employee of a dreaded bureaucracy, convinced she would harm them. Her job was only to protect the public. Nothing she did was personal, but rather protective of the environment and the U.S. Meat supply.

"I'm not willing to say anything until I'm certain. There is no need to panic and Miss Tangier is working with me to get my herd tested before round up."

When she put the ban on selling his cattle, Cody had been livid, but here he was defending her. Shocked gripped her as she listened to him, warmth spiraling through her.

"It's a damn conspiracy," the man screamed. "Don't be fooled into thinking they're here to help you. The government will shut your business down and ruin you. Our best bet is to run this woman out of town. After all, why are we listening to what the USDA says? They're just another bureaucracy."

The reporters shouted at her that she must have known what her father had been doing. Protecting him and their wealth. Funny, her father would never discuss his business, telling her he must guard the confidentiality of his clients and their interests.

A teenager about to enter college, all she understood was that he ran an investment firm, nothing more. Now she was once again being accused of ruining people. Even trying to help, people didn't appreciate what she did.

Beside her, Kyle tensed and his chair scooted back as he came to his feet, holding up his hand. "Stop. Listen to yourselves. You all know me and I've been taking care of your animals for years. In fact, I'm the one who suspected something was wrong with Cody's heifer and sent the tests off to the USDA. If the contamination spreads everyone's herds are in danger. We want to safeguard your livelihood and our beef."

Running his hand through his hair, Kyle said, "Now we've warned you. The way I see it there are two choices. Ignore our warnings when you see a heifer or a bull with suspicious behavior or you can call us. We're here to, run tests and keep the rest of your animals from catching this debilitating sickness. As a doctor, it's a simple choice, be aware or risk losing your entire herd."

Ryan moved to stand close to her.

Kyle and him exchanged a glance. "This meeting is adjourned. The doctor and myself will remain here for a few minutes to answer any questions you may have, unless someone gets out of line. Then we'll be gone."

His brothers, Drew and Jim closed in around her as if to shield her. They had her back. There was no reason to fear. Tears welled up in her eyes. No one ever safeguarded her. Never.

Not even when her mother was alive and her father in jail. Not even as a child. There had been no need until her father destroyed all their lives.

A little old man who had obviously been around for many years, walked up to the front. "Ma'am, we had an outbreak of this disease back in the forties. It decimated entire herds. Keep up the good work. Don't mind, none of these young fools. They haven't seen the destruction."

"Thank you," she said. "My intent is not to cause harm, but to stop an epidemic."

"And you will," he said and shuffled out the door, his legs bowed from riding horses for years.

Looking at Kyle, she smiled, her heart pounding in her chest. There was so much to like about this man, that it pained her to think of leaving. But for his safety, she would. "Thank you."

With a shrug of his shoulders, he shook his head. "These blockheads don't understand. Somewhere they got the notion that everyone is just out to screw em."

Turning back to his brothers, she shook her head, unable to believe they would defend her. "Thank you."

"For what?" Jim asked. "All you were doing is trying to inform the public. A couple of hot heads always ruin it for everyone."

Drew frowned. "Actually, I thought you handled that perfectly. Let me know when you get tired of working for the government and no longer want to be a vet. You've got a job anytime with me in the law office."

"Oh no," she said, remembering the many lawyers she dealt with in her father's case. Not only for him, but the U.S. attorney's office. "Animals are much safer than attorneys. They're easier to understand than you guys in suits. Thank you for having my back."

Standing beside her, Kyle grinned at her, creating a tingly sensation in her middle. "That's what my family does. We protect those we believe in."

"Just don't be stealing the clothes from my hot tub again," Cody said.

Holding her hands up, she shook her head and laughed. "I didn't. That was Kyle. But he said something about it being a payback."

Cody grinned. "Yeah, it was."

Part of her ached to belong to such a group. As a child, she longed for siblings, but in the end had no one, but her mother and father and the few aunts and uncles. But no one in her family believed in her and had her back. No one like the Lawrence boys.

CHAPTER 23

*L*ater that evening, after all of his brothers and his sister and Cody left, she sat drinking a glass of wine on the patio. Watching the moon rise in the sky while Kyle made sure all the animals in the clinic were fed and been taken out for the night.

This afternoon had been daunting. For a moment, she truly felt like the crowd wanted to pick her up, haul her out to her car, throw her in and tell her to get out of town.

As an agent of the USDA, she'd been warned there were times you needed to call for backup. Sometimes the situation called for more than one due to the security and vulnerability of the agents. If things grew worse, she would have to seek help.

Kyle's family surrounded her. The sheriff stood close to her and for Cody, someone injured in this debacle, to support her, brought a tear to her eye.

Her father's family and even her mother's all deserted her when they learned of the extent of what her father had done. Everyone did everything they could to distance themselves from his firm. No one wanted their name connected in any way with her father. No matter, he supported and given them money for many years.

And Kyle, warmth spread through her at how he stood and defended her. At first she feared Mr. Jones would come after her. But with charm boy standing beside her and the rest of the Lawrence brothers surrounding her, relief overwhelmed her.

Even thinking about Kyle, her chest squeezed and excitement filled her at the thought of being with him.

What did it feel like when you cared about a man? What did falling in love feel like? Never before did she have the opportunity to care for someone. Since Scott Gaston's downfall, she never experienced dating and relationships before now.

Gazing around at the small town, the lights shining in the darkness, her heart warmed. This little community was special. A place where you could put down roots and stay forever. But not a woman like Tempe.

Kyle was a wonderful man. A man any woman would be fortunate to fall in love with. All she wanted was to love him heart and soul, but she would be a danger. A danger that if uncovered would derail his life completely. No one deserved to live with the fear of discovery.

CHAPTER 24

*K*yle went up the stairs, knowing instinctively Tempe would be outside. Several nights he found her sitting on his patio peering out at the lights of Cupid, staring at the night sky, relaxing.

This afternoon's meeting had frightened the hell out of him. If those ranchers ever learned who she really was, they wouldn't run her out of town, they would commit the first public hanging in Cupid. Now he understood why she kept her identity a secret.

That damn David Jones would be lucky if he didn't hunt the man down and kick his butt. And that surprised him.

Normally a easy going, laid back guy, Kyle dealt with people by either teasing them until they smiled or handling them succinctly. David made the hair on the back of Kyle's neck stand straight up. It took every ounce of willpower to refrain from jumping off that platform with fists clenched towards David Jones.

Did he think Tempe was to blame for this disease? If the truth were known old man Smith's randy bull had a problem staying behind a fence and was the one they should be blaming. Ed Smith didn't keep the beast locked up and now the bull was spreading this infection with his rampant loins.

Or had been until he was told to separate him from the other cattle and fence him in.

Time that old bull was neutered. Unless he had Brucellosis. Then the only other option was putting him down.

Opening the door, he stepped out to see Tempe drinking a glass of wine and sitting gazing out into the darkness.

"Everyone taken care of for the night?" she asked.

"Yes. My technicians arrive early in the morning and handle the feeding and the walks."

"For such a small town, you seem to have a lot of business."

"I'm the only vet and my clients are loyal," he said.

More and more he realized how fortunate he was to own his practice. To live where he did. The people in the community supported him and entrusted him to care for their animals.

"Thanks for stepping in and helping me out today." Glancing up at him, her green eyes sparkling in the moonlight. "I'm just an employee carrying out her job and sometimes these people don't understand I don't make the rules and regulations."

There it was again, that phrase letting him know statues were important to her. Did she recognize how determined to show the world she followed the letter of the law?

"Have you always been so strict with regards to the rules?" he asked.

Her brows drew together and she gazed at him a startled expression on her lovely face. With her hand, she pushed back her auburn curls and his gut clenched. The urge to run his hands through her silken strands almost overwhelming him. They hadn't kissed since the night they made love. The night he found out she was a virgin.

Somehow he felt a sense of pride she had chosen him to be her first. Warmth flowed through him, even though feeling pleasure at being her first was ridiculous. Today he would have protected her at all costs.

"Until you mentioned it, I never gave it much thought. Before DWJ, I don't remember worrying too much about anything. After DWJ, I make certain I don't get into trouble."

"What is DWJ?"

A deep throaty chuckle came from her and he wanted to hear more of that sound. "It's my initials for Dad Went to Jail."

Setting down beside her, he picked up her hand. "You do realize that's why you're now a rules follower? The reason why everything is done according to the law."

Tilting her head sideways, she considered him. "Probably. But don't you see they would love to pin something on me and my dead mother showing the world we knew all along. Don't you think most people believed we were as culpable as my father? Now I have to prove I'm a law abiding citizen, before I never worried."

She was right. There had been speculation in the news as to whether or not the rest of his family were involved in the business. Thankfully, she'd been in school, but her mother...and then the suicide.

"Why do you think my mother killed herself?"

"Your mother couldn't take the stress any longer?"

"After she lost everything, including her reputation, she became despondent. Even I was not enough to keep her here on earth. Sometimes I think she did it so I would inherit her money to go to school. Sometimes I think she just wore down and couldn't take the pain another day. Either way, it hurt."

Lifting her hand to his lips, he kissed the back of it. "Someday I hope this is all behind you and you're living a life filled with love and promise and happiness."

All he wanted to do was bring joy into her world. Make her forget what happened or at the very least, give her contentment and joy that would ease her loss.

A tear rolled down her cheek. "Dammit Kyle, I've been trying not to like you too much, but you surprise me and make me like you every time we're together. Turn off the charm, charm boy."

With a laugh he shook his head. "You're the first woman who has ever called me that and frankly, I like it."

Leaning her head against his shoulder, she sighed. "Could that be because it fits?"

The name did fit. All his life, he managed to smile and talk people into what he wanted. Now he had everything but a wife and family of his own. Until Tempe he hadn't really considered a wife and family, but now...Glancing at the woman sitting next to him, he wondered what life with her would be like.

Sliding over in the seat, she got as close to him as possible and gazed out at the night sky. "Do you ever wonder what is beyond those stars."

"Nope," he said and brushed back her hair away from her face. As he leaned down, his lips inches from her own all he could think about was kissing her. "There is too much here on earth that intrigues me to worry what is behind the heavens."

Right now what intrigued him sat beside him admiring the twinkles of light shining up from Cupid. He wanted Tempe, like he needed his next breath, like he needed sunshine and fresh air. Like he needed to be accepted and loved.

His mouth covered hers. The taste of wine and sweetness left him wanting to devour her lips. This afternoon fear gripped him at the way David Jones had riled the crowd up against her. Afraid he finally stepped up and taken over.

Tonight, he longed to find his way back into her arms, back in his bed.

Breaking the kiss her eyes opened slowly and he seemed to lose himself in her emerald gaze. "Come to bed with me," he whispered against her mouth. "Let me show you the joy of lovemaking."

An ache spread through his chest and he waited, hoping she

would not turn him down. After today he needed to feel her strong arms around him. Tonight he needed to feel her safe and secure in his embrace.

Slowly, she smiled.

"Come on charm boy. We don't know what tomorrow will bring, but we've got all night."

CHAPTER 25

"*H*ow do you plan on showing me this joy you mentioned?"

"I'm going to ravish your sweet, beautiful body until you're begging me to stop."

"Kyle" she groaned against his lips.

Placing his mouth next to her ear, he nuzzled her neck and earlobe, his tongue sliding across her flesh. A shudder rippled through her, and he smiled, knowing he affected her as much as she was him.

Standing, he took her by the hand and pulled her into his quarters, shutting and locking the door behind him. This afternoon the city and the ranchers had mistreated her, but tonight he would give her satisfaction.

Biting her lip, her eyes wide with expectation and something that looked like desire they stood just inside. Anticipating what was about to happen, before he freed the hunger for Tempe raging through him.

"Tempe," he gasped.

She met his gaze head on, her breathing quick and shallow. With sudden realization, he knew she wanted this as much as he did, and her eagerness sent him over the edge. Taking her by the hand, he walked into the bedroom, pulling her inside, shutting the door.

Pushing her up against the wooden panel, his body covered hers, pressing into her soft voluptuous curves, his rock-solid erection snug against her womanly mound. His mouth came down hard on her full lips expressing his need.

Moaning deep in her throat, he relished the sound. While he caressed her luscious lips, his hands were busy removing her USDA shirt over her head, needing to reach her skin, to touch that satiny flesh.

Abruptly, she broke the seal of their mouths and yanked the offending garment over her head, and he tossed his own polo.

"Let me run my hands over your chest," she said.

"Yes," he whispered, barely able to talk, his need for her so great.

Her fingers trailed from his neck down to his waist, where she unsnapped his pants. Leaning down, he pulled off his boots and socks. With a thrust his jeans slid to the floor, she kicked off her shoes and tugged her pants off. They stood in front of the door naked, their breath constricted, lost in the building heat between them.

Simultaneously, they swayed toward each other, reaching out at the same time, as he dragged her mouth to his, wanting to consume her full lips. A moan rent the air, and he was shocked to realize the groan came from him as he crushed her mouth beneath his, longing guiding him.

Breaking the seal of their kiss, he leaned his forehead against hers. "Do you know how much I want you?"

And he did. Today when he deemed her safety had been in jeopardy, he realized he would do whatever he needed to protect her. Watching her talking to those ungrateful bastards he'd never felt more connected to a woman.

Tempe Tangier intrigued him more than anyone he ever

dated. Yet they weren't really even dating. All they were doing was working together. Would she go out with him once this was over? Would she agree to let him see her again?

"I think so," she said, her voice soothing, her breath whispery.

"No one has ever created such heat like you. No one has made me want to fight heaven and earth to be with you," he promised as he walked backwards to the bed.

A shiver went through her.

"Are you cold? Let me warm you." He pulled her down with him to the bed.

"Not cold. Hot with need for you," she panted, her fingertips running down his chest, his stomach, to his manhood. As she wrapped her hand around him, he groaned the sound echoing in the room. Full to bursting with need for her as she massaged him until his blood throbbed with heat.

"Let me fix that for you because I ache with want for you," he said as he gripped her head, holding her mouth hostage, his fingers tangling in her hair, not letting her escape his kiss.

Then he slid his hands down her neck to her shoulders and further until he reached her chest. Cupping her pale globes, he released her lips from his and bent down to lift the weight of her breast to his lips.

Gently, he pulled on her nipple, sucking as much of her into his mouth as he could, as she bucked wildly against him, her moans loud in the room. As her hands moved to his head, trapping him against her breasts, trying to give him more access to her body, her breathing ragged and harsh.

With a gentle stroke he trailed his hand down her body, skimming over her flat stomach, down until his caress touched her intimate folds, and she whimpered his name.

"Kyle."

Plucking his lips from her nipple, he stared as desire filled her eyes, and she gazed at him with longing.

"Your skin feels like silk or satin," he said as he delved inside her center. Slowly, he stroked her, watching her face change. Gripping the quilt in her fists, his fingers teased her until she squirmed and moaned.

Tightening around him, she screamed, shuddering as her passion-filled eyes stared straight into his soul. Touching him like no one had ever done before.

Quickly he reached into the night stand and pulled out a condom. With a rip he opened the package and sheathed himself with the rubber. Smiling, he parted her legs with his.

Astonished, they fit perfectly together, her breasts against his chest, her hips supporting him, his shaft nestled between the juncture of her thighs, right where he belonged. Unable to hold back any longer, he entered her in a single swift movement.

"You feel great," she murmured. "Filling me up."

"Tempe," he groaned in the semi-dark room.

Staring into her eyes, he believed they were joined as one as he moved inside her, stroking her, loving her. Clutching his back, she clung to him as together they rode the waves of passion, holding onto one another.

This woman had taken on the challenges of a father who devastated the family fortune, become a vet, and this afternoon faced a roomful of unhappy ranchers. She'd beaten them all and had no idea of how strong and capable she was. A compressing spiral of need consumed him, and as much as he wished he could last longer, he couldn't.

"Kyle," Tempe cried as she convulsed with pleasure.

With a guttural cry, he slammed into her body, shuddering his release. No matter what happened in their future, he would always remember tonight.

Rolling them to their sides, tucking her tight against his body, his heart was pounding, his pulse racing. Glancing up at him, her eyes were half lidded, spent from their lovemaking and he reached down and kissed her on the lips.

"What a wonderful way to end a crappy day," she said. "For just a few moments, you made me forget everything."

"You're welcome," he said and wondered how did he continue to live his life without her by his side.

The thought surprised him and he quickly pushed it away. Soon this epidemic would be behind them and she would be on her way. But would she go out with him when this was over? Could they become more than just coworkers? Could they become lovers and friends?

CHAPTER 26

*T*he next morning, the calls began. Ranchers who had listened to their warnings grasped the risks involved if one of their cows became ill. Suddenly they were booked for most of the day.

Packing their bags, she looked over at him, warmth filling her. The thought crossed her mind of spending the rest of her life by his side and then the logical part of her, reminded her of her past.

How the press would make his life miserable if they learned the truth about who she was. As much as she wanted to be with Kyle, it could never happen. Staying with him would put him at risk.

Over the years she'd mastered how to put her emotions away, pushing aside her feelings she locked them away. This was a brief moment in time, nothing more. Like a monkey on her back, the past would never allow this relationship to be anything else, ever.

"Come on," he said grabbing her hand. "Let's go."

"Yes, we've got a busy day," she said. "If this keeps up, I may have to call for back up."

"Let's see as many ranches as we can," he said, reaching down and giving her a quick kiss on the lips. "Tonight when we return home, I'll give you another lesson in lovemaking."

A sigh escaped her. Life with this man would be fun and interesting and that frightened her. Already she could tell her heart was quickly becoming involved and she was falling in love with the handsome charmer. For his own protection, she couldn't stay.

"Did I pass last night?" she asked teasing him.

"Absolutely, you received an A, but I think there is always room for improvement. So tonight we'll work a little harder at getting your grade up," he said. "You're such a smart student and have the ability to make an A plus."

Shaking her head she laughed. "You are a goofus, charm boy. Now let's go to work. We have an epidemic to bring under control."

For the next four hours, they worked tirelessly checking cattle, drawing blood and giving the ranchers advice on how to keep the possible infection from spreading. Their biggest concerns were the two ranches next to old man Smith's randy bull, that they knew had the disease.

That would be their last stop of the day. Where they would inform him, the results of the tests and the need to euthanize the diseased animal.

No, Mr. Smith wouldn't be happy, they both recognized he would be upset, but unfortunately that was unavoidable.

At the Callahan ranch, they worked together. Kyle talking to the rancher while Tempe took the blood from the animal.

Poking the animal gently with a cattle prod, to get the heifer moving into the chute, where Tempe could draw the necessary blood work. All part of the testing exam needed to determine whether the cow had Brucellosis.

"How many calves has she aborted?" Kyle asked taking notes.

"Two in the last six months. This animal is not eating like she should or putting on weight," the rancher informed them.

"Come on, girl," she said, pushing her, avoiding standing directly behind the cow. Stepping into a hole, her ankle buckled and she felt herself falling.

Trying to regain her balance, she fell forward at the same time she saw the animals hoof coming towards her chest. Turning to the side to avoid almost certain death, the kick hit her just below her breasts.

Like a knife plunging into her, knocking the breath from her as the sharp claw propelled her backwards.

With a wham, she landed on her back and gasped, fearing she would never suck air again.

"Tempe," Kyle screamed. Immediately, he was by her side. "Where are you hurt?"

Everything moved in slow motion as she watched the old man, shove the animal with the cattle prod propelling her into the squeeze chute and locking it behind her.

"Is she all right?" he asked, standing over her, gazing at her with a worried expression on his face.

She couldn't talk. She couldn't draw air into her lungs. Her chest burned and radiated with agony and she wheezed, panic seizing her.

"Relax," Kyle said in his doctor's voice. "Relax. That heifer knocked the air out of you. Slowly try to take a deep breath."

Pain spasmed through her ribcage and she moaned, but did feel her lungs filling once again. A searing ache emanated through her chest area and she couldn't move. Not yet. Not until this throbbing eased just a little.

"Let me look where she kicked you," Kyle said.

Barely able to breathe as she focused on trying to ease the , she couldn't stop him, if she wanted to.

He pulled her polo shirt out of her jeans and then lifted it up keeping her bra covered. At this moment searing, anguish radiated from her ribs and she honestly didn't care that the old man was getting an eye full. Right now, she hurt too bad to think of modesty.

Bending over, the older man's grimace was enough to let her know the sight wasn't pretty. "Oh my."

"Shit," he said. "The claw got you good. Looks like it's already starting to bruise."

"I..m...all right," she said with a wheeze.

"Like hell you are," he said. "Let me check your ribs."

When he placed his hand on her ribcage even though he was gentle, she screamed as he touched the area of the kick.

"That's it," he said. "I'm taking you to the ER."

No, she didn't want to go to the hospital. Whenever her records were checked she had an irrational fear that somehow they would learn her past. Find out her real identity and notify the press.

"No. Take the heifer's blood," she said with a moan.

"No," he said.

"Damn it I'm not leaving until you take her blood. Give me a moment and I'll get up and do it myself. We didn't come all this way out here for me to be kicked for nothing," Tempe demanded.

Right now they needed to learn if they had another case and didn't have time to come back out here and do this again. There were other cattle waiting.

His mouth thinned and he gritted his teeth. "Has anyone ever told you how stubborn you are?"

"No," she said, her voice barely a whisper. Her stubbornness was probably why she was still alive and not sniveling away in a corner somewhere. "Just take the blood."

The owner who had been standing off to the side, glanced at Kyle. "She's right. Take what you need and then I'll put this heifer in a separate pasture away from the other animals. The sooner you collect the blood, the sooner you can take Dr. Tangier to see a doctor."

"Were there any others you had concerns about?" Tempe said, trying to sit, grimacing from the throbbing torment.

There was no time for an injury. No time for emergency room visits and yet all she could think about was a possible cracked rib or pierced lung.

"No, she's the only one I know of. Miss Tangier, I'm really sorry she got you with her hoof."

"One of the many dangers of this job," Tempe gasped as pain pounded through her. While she didn't want to seek medical help, maybe it was a good idea to be examined. As a vet even she knew the dangers of an injury like this.

In less than five minutes, he had the specimen from the animal. Labeling the test tube with the ranch name and the identification number of the heifer, he carefully packed the sample away.

Sitting on the ground not far away, her breathing labored, Tempe realized she had to go to the ER.

"Let me help you up," he said, reaching down as he and the old man tried to lift her to her feet instead of pulling her.

For a moment she thought she would pass out from the palpitating ache. Taking small shallow breaths, she gazed at the owner, her vision blurry.

"Just as soon as we know the results, I'll either come out to see or call you to tell you what we found. In the meantime, don't let any animal near her. Even a dog is susceptible to this infection. No animals, no one," she instructed.

"Thanks," the rancher said. "Go get those ribs checked out."

"I think I'll be okay," she said. "Give me a little time to rest."

With every breath, her lungs tightened, like a knife stabbing her in the chest.

"We're going to the ER," Kyle commanded, placing his arm around her and helping her walk across the land to the car. Leaning her head on his shoulder, depending on him for help, knowing this was not how she planned on spending her day with him, she sighed.

"Why did I have to trip," she said. "I'm such a klutz."

"Accidents occur," he said. "Thank goodness you weren't alone."

"That would have been bad," she said, trying to keep the groan from out of her voice.

As they reached the car, he carefully sat her inside and pulled the seat belt across her chest, tears welled up at the touch of the strap. No matter what, she needed to go to the emergency room.

"Maybe you're right. Maybe we should go to the hospital."

A scowl crossed his face as he stared out the windshield.. "No choice. We're headed there now."

CHAPTER 27

*K*yle watched as they wheeled her back into the ER. The small hospital was quiet and unless another emergency walked in, he doubted she would be in there long.

Sinking down into one of the chairs, he placed his elbows on his knees and his head in the palm of his hands. What a scary day.

In veterinary school they warned about getting kicked in the chest. A hard enough kick, landing in the right place on your chest could stop your heart. When he saw her falling, terror exploded through him and he couldn't reach her fast enough. Terrified when that hoof landed on her chest and sent her flying back.

Thank goodness the rancher had settled the heifer down and pushed her completely into the chute, while he focused on Tempe.

Rubbing his palms across his face, he contemplated what happened and his chest ached at the thought of her being seriously hurt. No question she would be sore, bruised and in pain for several days, but what if she'd broken her ribs. What if she punctured a lung.

As a vet, he understood the possibilities of what she could of injured. Fear spread through him and he jumped up out of his seat and began to pace the floor.

That was Tempe back in the examining room. With a determined stride he went over to the check in desk. "Is there anyway I can go back and be with Miss Tangier?"

"Are you family?" he swallowed the urge to lie on the tip of his tongue. "No."

"Sorry sir, you'll need to wait. Give me a few minutes and I'll go talk to her, " she said and went back to her work.

Tempe waited in the exam room, hurting, frightened, all alone. A woman he had come to know, since the night he danced around the Cupid statue. A woman that he'd seen that heifer knock senseless sending terror gripping his heart.

Like a slap to his face, he stopped and gazed at the swinging doors where they rolled her through.

A warm sensation flowed through his veins and he closed his eyes at the sudden realization. "Oh my," he said out loud in the empty waiting room. "Oh my."

Just the thought of her warmed his chest and filled him with hope, with promise and something he hadn't experienced in a long long time. He'd fallen in love with Scott Gaston's daughter. He'd fallen in love with the caring woman. He'd fallen in love with a woman he considered his equal. A strong woman with an intelligent, sharp mind now held his heart hostage.

And now he was uneasy about her health.

No, he didn't mean to fall in love. In fact, he had not been searching for someone - but Tempe was the smartest, stubbornness, person he knew and she made him happy. Made him a better vet, a better lover, even a better man.

Pacing the small area, he halted in front of the front desk. "Have you checked on her?"

"Not yet," the woman said, glancing at him like he was becoming a burden.

Taking a deep breath, he gave her his best smile, leaned down close to her and said, "I'm sure working at a hospital, you're very busy. No, we aren't related yet, but she's my fiancé and I'm concerned about her. Could you let me go back there for a moment to reassure me she's doing fine?."

"Are you trying to get me fired?"

"Never," he said. 'But if they did, you would have a job at my clinic. All I need is five minutes with her."

The need to see her beautiful face, check and see she was really going to be okay overwhelmed him and if this clerk didn't let him go back, he'd force his way to Tempe.

With a frown, the girl glanced at her watch. "It's now three forty-five. You've got until three fifty one and if you're not back out here, I'm calling security."

Kyle smiled and started running towards the door. "Thank you," he called. "Yes, you have a job if you need it."

Pushing through the doors, he soon found her lying in a bed, her eyes shut.

Just seeing her confirmed everything his heart had been telling him. For a moment, his throat clogged with the awareness he loved this woman. Loved her smile, her sense of right and wrong and her belief in the rules, though he hoped to soften her stand on that a little.

"Hey, you doing all right?" he asked, worried she lay so still and lifeless.

"No, it hurts to breathe," she said. "I'm so stupid. I got careless and in a matter of seconds, that cow let me know she was none too happy with me."

"We all make mistakes," he said, picking up her hand. "Has the doctor been in yet?"

Her color was pale, her face drawn and she appeared to still have a lot of discomfort.

"Oh yes, now they're getting ready to take me to X-ray."

"They let you come back?"

"Bribed the lady up front. She only gave me five minutes."

"Still using that charm," she said with a smile that turned into a grimace.

How had the word charm become such an endearment, but it had and warmth rushed through him. What could he say, she was right, he used his charm to get to her. All he wanted was Tempe.

There was so much he needed to say to her, but this was not the most romantic place in the world to confess his feelings. Now was not the time to share with her that he loved her.

"Tempe, I'm aching for you, but if I'm not back by three fifty one, she'll call security."

Reaching down he kissed her on the temple. "Tell them to give you a shot of morphine. You need it."

"Like hell, I do," she said. "That stuff will knock me out."

If he were her doctor, she would already have some pain medication.

"Which would be for the best," he said. "Rest."

"Charm boy you better leave, before they send in the janitor to kick you out."

At her comment, he laughed, his heart warming. How had the five minutes gone by so quickly. "See you soon."

Running back down the hall and out through the door, he realized he didn't want her leaving town. Dr. Tempe Tangier, needed to stay right here, be his partner in business and in life. For the first time he wanted to ask a woman to be his wife.

The image of the Cupid statue came into his mind and he shook his head. No, it couldn't be because of that damn superstition. It couldn't be true. Yet, Tempe was the first woman he laid eyes on after doing the Cupid stupid dance.

CHAPTER 28

Several days later, Tempe moved gingerly around a heifer, knowing she couldn't withstand another kick. Since she'd walked out of the ER, Kyle treated her like she was made of glass. And while he carefully watched over her felt endearing, she knew she had to grow stronger - quickly.

"Done," she said and stepped away from the heifer. They opened the chute and the cow ran out into the pasture. "Keep her isolated until the results come back, which should be tomorrow."

"Yes, every evening they let us know the outcome from the tests and then the next day we take care of the cattle who are ill or deliver good news to the rancher," Kyle said.

"We are finding fewer and fewer infected. It's mainly been around our patient zero," Tempe said, recognizing that soon her time here would come to an end and she would have to leave.

Kyle put down old man Smith's bull the day after she was injured, the day she couldn't move. Yes, they had to euthanize several more cows, but the epidemic appeared to be slowing. Hopefully tonight they would learn that zero cattle had tested infected and in a few days this episode could be considered over.

Packing her backpack she turned to the rancher. "We'll talk to you tomorrow."

Carefully she picked up her backpack.

"Give me that," Kyle said as he grabbed her bag.

"I could carry it," she said. "I have to get better."

"Not today you don't," he said, walking beside her.

When they reached the car, he opened the door for her. They'd come in her car, hoping it would be easier for her to crawl in and out of. Yet, any time she moved, she hurt.

Sinking easily down onto the seat, she smiled at him. "Thank you, but can we please go back to the clinic."

After several hours she seemed to run out of energy. Yes, she was healing, but her ribs and chest were black, and purple with a touch of green. But she was lucky that heifer didn't pack enough punch to break her ribs only bruise them.

"That's where we're headed," he said strolling around to the driver's side.

Bouncing along the dirt road, she didn't know if she would pass out or become car sick or both. In the fifteen minutes it took to reach paved highway, Kyle kept looking over at her, but she did her best to keep her chin up and anticipate the bumps.

Kyle's cell phone rang and he answered the call, making her even more nervous. In her car, the bluetooth didn't automatically connect to his phone only hers.

"Dr. Lawrence," he said.

"What? Why? Did they say why they were here?" he glanced over at Tempe and a prickle of alarm scurried down her spine.

"She's here with me and we're on our way back to the clinic now," he told whoever he was speaking to on the phone. "Tell them we'll be there in about ten minutes. Thanks."

Disconnecting, he frowned and looked over at her. "Did you send for back up?"

"Back up what are you talking about?" she asked confused.

"Gloria said ten USDA people arrived with a big lab truck."

She cursed. "That fool didn't listen. Specifically, I told my boss I was fine and didn't need help. Obviously he didn't heed my instructions."

Laying her head back against the seat rest, she sighed. "Just get me there, so I can start dealing with these fools. You watch and see, they're going to want to shut down the counties herds."

CHAPTER 29

*W*hen Kyle walked into his office, he found the USDA had more or less moved into his clinic. His staff scurried around, relief etched across his office manager's face the moment she saw he was back.

Tempe hurried over to a man wearing a red polo. "Dan, you didn't tell me you were coming. And why did you bring the team?"

"We're dealing with a Brucellosis epidemic," he said, giving her a look that made the hair on Kyle's neck bristle. From what he could tell, Tempe was probably a genius and the man was talking down to her.

"According to my reports, we haven't had a contaminated sample since we eliminated Patient Zero."

Nodding his head, Dan said bluntly, "The team and I are going to quarantine the herds."

The egotistical jerk wanted control of the situation.

"Why?" Tempe asked. "Do you realize the burden you're putting on these ranchers? Do you realize how many you're going to wipe out?"

Kyle regardedTempe as she fought for what she believed in and wanted her to fight for him the same way.

"Do you want our region to be the one responsible for the next outbreak that destroys the cattle industry in the US?"

Drawing back her shoulders, a ripple of pain crossed Tempe's face. She raised her head and stared at the man directly. Oh, the battle was on.

"Give me your reasoning for placing a quarantine on this area?"

The man gave a little laugh like she was being ridiculous. "Five cows tested positive for the disease."

"Only four and the bull was patient zero," she said.

The man's eyes narrowed and Kyle realized he did not appreciate her questioning his authority, but yet she was standing up for the owners here in town. That made his heart swell with love and warmth. If those bastards could behold her now, they would never question her integrity again.

"All four are from different ranches in the area."

"The three heifers were infected by a bull who broke down a fence to reach them," she said gasping.

While he was damn proud of her, Kyle recognized she was running out of strength and energy.

"All three ranches butted up against patient zero's ranch. All three have agreed to test their cattle. We've spent the last two days checking other ranches where owners reported suspicious animals. So far no positive test results."

Kyle tried to hide the smile on his face. Looking around the crowded room, his staff and even a few clients, watched the drama unfold before their eyes. This little scene would be spread all over Cupid by evening.

"In the interest of the beef industry all the herds in this region should be tested."

Tempe shrugged a pained expression crossed her face. She was hurting, but continued on. "Okay, if that's what you think we should do, but that will devastate the department's budget for this year. Since we know who started this epidemic, as long as he didn't get out and go visiting ten miles away, why should the rancher up the road be subject to your debilitating actions?"

The red polo shirt clearly said, Dan Miller, USDA embroidered in white lettering. As he glared at her, he said, "Due to your injuries, I'm hereby relieving you from this investigation and sending you back to Austin."

Shaking her head, she said, "No. I'm staying here and fighting for the small everyday cattleman. Fire me, but I will still stay here and give them advice on how to end this quarantine. I promised them that if they helped with the epidemic, there would be no holds placed on their stock. Now, you're here and the first thing you want to do is stop them from selling their beef. Which makes the owners think once again, we're out to get them. No, Dan, I'm going to work with the locals to stop you."

Shock rippled through Kyle. The girl who wanted everything done by the letter of the law, was fighting for the people in their small community and he'd never felt prouder of her than at this moment.

He loved this woman and today, just proved everything he believed true about her. When this madness settled down, he would confess his love and ask her to marry him. The hell with her father and his terrible crime. His daughter was gold.

"Kyle," she said, turning with a grimace on her face. "Would you please contact the local cattleman's association and tell them we need an urgent meeting to discuss how to end the USDA's quarantine on the cattle in this area."

"You can't do that," Dan said emphatically. "You work for the USDA."

With an evil smile, her brows rose. "Oh, I'll be filing a grievance against you and then if necessary, I'll be handing you my resignation. You're not going to bankrupt these cattlemen without a huge fight on your hands. Are you ready?"

Resisting the urge to chuckle out loud, Kyle had to turn away. Dan's face was close to the same color as his shirt. His eyes grew large, like he couldn't believe she'd just stood up to him.

"Kyle, invite some news crews and a couple of reporters to attend our little gathering. The press needs to know what's going on."

The woman was bluffing and Kyle stared at the growing panic in her boss's eyes. But Kyle knew she would never be around a TV camera or a reporter ever again.

"Stop!" Dan yelled.

CHAPTER 30

a week later, Tempe watched as the crew pulled out with the trailer with Dan on board. Relief flowed over her and once again, she could return back to her job. Yet part of her wasn't ready to leave.

Once the rig filled with big shots rolled into town, not a single cow tested positive. While it had been a huge waste of taxpayers money, which she would include in her report, at least she won her fight about the quarantine.

Only one herd remained quarantined and that was Mr. Smith's cattle. Even there, she believed they caught all the infected cases and sadly the randy bull had gone to greener pastures in the sky.

Cody's herd checked out disease free. And even the other two ranches who the bull went a courting were clear of any infection.

This afternoon, as soon as Kyle finished with his patients, she would tell him goodbye and get on the road to home. There she would pack her bags and escape for four days to the beaches in Port Aransas.

Not the sparkling white beaches of the Caribbean, but the

cheapest beach vacation she could take and still feel the sand between her toes.

"Miss Tangier?" she heard a man say her name and glanced up from packing the trunk of her car. A sizzle of fear trickled down her spine.

Her nemesis from the town hall meeting stared at her in the driveway. "Good morning, Mr. Jones?"

The shrunken cowboy stopped in front of her and took his hat off. Nervously, he swallowed as she gazed at the little man. "I'm here today to apologize. My sister was sitting in Dr. Lawrence's waiting room the day you stood up to the USDA. When she got home, she told me I was an ass for treating you the way I did. That you really did have the best interests of the ranchers at heart."

Tempe sighed and smiled at him, trying to make him feel a little more at ease, though he had been rude and terrifying.

His head dipped and then he raised it, his eyes locked on hers. "I want to apologize for my vulgar behavior that day in the town hall. At the time I was so scared my cattle would bankrupt me. All of my money is tied up in that herd. If my animals were quarantined thirty years of struggle would go down the drain."

This was the reason she fought for the ranchers. This was the reason she probably would lose her job. But in some small way when she helped others, she hoped to repay for what her father had done, it was worth the sacrifice.

"You and every other rancher in this area. Apology accepted."

"Thank you, ma'am. Thanks for standing up to those government officials. It means a lot."

"You're welcome," she said, smiling and holding out her hand.

The man twirled his hat in his hands trying to hide their shaking.

Taking her hand in his, he shook it.

"Mr. Jones, I wish you the best of luck with your cattle. Let's hope this is all behind us now."

"Anytime you want to come back to Cupid, please look me up and say hello."

A smile crossed her face. "Only if I'm not coming back for work reasons."

He grinned. "Agreed. Have a safe trip home."

"Thank you, Mr. Jones."

The little old man limped away and she shut the trunk. Now all she needed to do was tell Kyle bye. And that was the part she dreaded.

This time with him while stressful had also been some of the most magical time in her life. If only her past was a normal one, not a family that made the national headlines, she wouldn't leave.

The thought of saying goodbye to her charm boy, made her throat tighten. Since the day of the accident, he had taken care of her. That first night he even bathed her. Just thinking of the way he treated her like a piece of cherished china brought tears to her eyes.

Kyle Lawrence was the kind of man she dreamed of spending forever with. The kind of man she wanted children with. To wake up beside each morning, kiss goodnight each night. At any moment her cover could be blown, the past could come roaring at her, sucking her back into the spotlight that she wanted to avoid at all costs.

No man, no children, no one. Not even herself should have to live with cameras following your every move, dragging your name through the mud, speculating as to what role you played or if there was money stashed away in an overseas account.

The only hidden stash Tempe Tangier had were the Milky Way bars she hoarded. The possibility of her losing her job over her actions with her boss were pretty darn good or at the very least a reprimand. Right now that no longer mattered. Leaving Kyle behind along with a chunk of her heart was her focus. And frankly, she didn't know how she would get through the next few days.

Somewhere in all the drama, she'd fallen in love with the big hunk of a cowboy. Fallen in love and knew that he didn't deserve a wife with a daunting past.

Wiping her eyes, trying to bring her emotions under control, she walked back into the clinic.

"Miss Tangier," his receptionist said. "We were all hoping you wouldn't leave us."

"No, I'm going home and then spend some days gazing at the ocean."

"Oh?" Gloria said. "Where are you going?"

Tempe remembered all the places she spent summers in her life and then proudly said, "I'm going to vacation in Port Aransas. I'm renting a one bedroom at the Sand Dunes Condominiums for four nights. After the last couple of weeks, I need the rest and relaxation."

"Have a wonderful trip and watch out for the sand sharks," Gloria told her and with a sinking heart, Tempe realized she would miss the ladies in his practice.

"Thanks," she said.

Just then Kyle stepped out of an exam room. Without a word he took her by the arm and led her upstairs. As the man she loved dragged her along with him, quietly. As they reached the apartment, he closed the door and turned towards her.

"Don't leave," he said leading her to the couch. "Since college, my dating life has been sparse, simply because I never met a woman that interested me. The two of us, we got off to a rocky start, but with you, I've met my match. There is nothing that we can't talk about. There's been fun and laughter during one of the worst crisis in Cupid."

Pausing, he took a deep breath, still holding her hands, gazing into her eyes.

"The time we've been together were tough ones, but I enjoy being with you. Though the day you got hurt, frightened ten years off my life. Seeing you lying on the ground, struggling to breathe I have never been so afraid. At that moment, I realized how much you brightened my life, how much I love you." Kyle ran his hand through his hair. "I love you more than I can say. Stay with me, marry me and spend your life here working in the hospital doing what we love."

Stunned, she stared at him, wanting so badly to say yes. His proposal was like tempting a diabetic with chocolate cake. Stay here with the man she loved and devote her days being happy, creating a family, being in a great community or be alone.

The idea of news trucks rolling down the streets of Cupid filled her mind. She imagined them parked right outside the clinic or the school or their home waiting for one of them to step out. Why would she do this to the people she cared about and wanted to protect?

Her heart pounded inside her chest and she wanted to scream at the unfairness. Though Kyle had her heart, she knew it was in his best interest to give him up.

With a cry, she rose. "Oh, please no, I can't. You know I can't. Marriage will never happen for me."

The crumpled expression on his face, ripped open her heart, she couldn't wait another minute. Grabbing her purse, she had to get out of here before she gave in. "Please, I can't."

Hurrying out the door, she ran down the stairs, ignoring the shocked expressions from the staff. Tears streamed down her face, as she sprinted out the door and jumped in her car.

Time to return to her empty, lonely life.

CHAPTER 31

*T*wo days later Kyle looked up to see his brothers, Jim and Drew march into Kyle's office. They didn't bother knocking, but rather walked in and shut the door behind them.

Gazing at the two of them he frowned. "Is this the firing squad coming to take me away?"

"No, we're here to do an intervention. A what happened to our brother intervention."

"What the hell are you talking about?" Kyle said frowning.

So he'd been drunk the last two nights. The first night Ryan escorted him out of the town square where he stood fully clothed cursing a blue streak at the statue. Never in his wildest dreams had he meant to fall for Tempe. She stormed into his world and shaken him to his core, taking his heart with her when she left.

It felt like all the sunshine disappeared, leaving him a broken man. All the charm he depended upon all his life, she must have packed it in her suitcases and taken it back to Austin.

"Ryan called us and told us he found you drunk in the town square, screaming at that piece of granite that you didn't want to fall in love."

Swallowing, he glanced away. "There is no privacy in this town."

"Then one of your staff phoned us and said even the animals are starting to quiver around you."

What could he say, he had been a little difficult these days. Blowing up when normally he praised his people. The worried expressions on their face, just pissed him off even more.

"The last and final straw was when you didn't show up for our dinner last night."

Oh crap! In his drunken state he missed Jim and Shadow's engagement party. His oldest brother was getting married and instead gotten drunk and thrown water filled surgical gloves off the balcony. Why? It was better than tossing glass. A lot less clean-up.

Putting his palms over his face, he rubbed it trying to hide his expression.

"Wow, sorry man," he said.

"What the hell is wrong with you?" Drew asked.

Stopping, he stared at his younger brother who had yet to dance around the fountain. "You don't have the right to say a word to me. Until you strip down naked and become vulnerable and have your heart battered by that boy in a diaper, you have no right to ask me what's wrong."

Drew gave a little half smile. "The judge frowns when you abandon a case."

Jumping up from behind his desk, Kyle was ready to fight someone, anyone. "No more excuses. It's your turn to face that demon statue, find a woman and let her crush your soul. When I did the dance, I didn't believe love would happen to me. After all, I wasn't looking for the happily ever after. Didn't really care about finding a wife, but oh no, that damn statue brought a girl right to my front door."

"Why aren't you marrying her?" Drew asked. "Seems a simple enough solution."

Those were fighting words. He almost begged her to marry him and instead she ran crying from the clinic, hauling her sweet little ass away as fast as her car would go. And it hurt. Bone crushing pain.

"Is love ever simple? How many times you been in love? We know you've experienced enough lust for all of us, but who has broken your heart?" Kyle shouted.

"Hey, I've experienced heartache before," Drew replied.

"Oh yeah, when?"

Drew sat back in his chair and frowned. "So I like the ladies. Not everyone is ready for marriage and babies."

"Well, I didn't think I was either." No way was the Cupid statue going to affect him. He was immune to love or so he believed. Until a smart intelligent woman quickly proved him wrong.

Warily, Kyle glanced over at his brother Jim. "You're being awfully quiet."

Across the desk from him, Jim laughed. "Funny, Cody had almost the same talk with me just a couple of weeks ago. Sitting here I'm thinking what convinced me to go after Shadow. Maybe because I realized my life would be nothing without her. Shadow makes me happy. She's ditzy and fun and more loving than I deserve. Swallow your dang pride and go after the woman and ask her to marry you."

Kyle's frustration was mounting and about to go off like a volcano. Seldom he lost his cool. Seldom he got angry. Right now he was ready to explode.

"Do you think I'm stupid? I asked her to marry me," he said all the vexation spilling over. "Tempe turned me down. Then she ran out the door."

The room grew quiet.

Drew glanced at him. "Do you know why?"

"Yes, I understand exactly the way her logical brain was working. The very reason she said no, but if I told you, I'd have to kill you."

The two brothers stared at each other and Kyle watched them and sighed. Could she be right? Was he not thinking clearly about the consequences of marrying Scott Gaston's daughter?

Bitting his lip, Jim said in that elder brother voice he seldom used anymore. "We're you're brothers. Why won't she marry you?"

Like a rock, he sank back down in the chair and put his hands on his face again. "Tempe Tangier is actually Tempe Gaston, Scott Gaston's daughter."

"I knew I'd seen her face before," Jim said glancing at Drew.

"The Scott Gaston. The one that ran the largest ponzi scheme in the history of the United States?"

"None other," Drew said with a sigh. "After the trial and her mother's death, she changed her name and moved from the east coast to get away from all the publicity. She doesn't want to drag a husband and children into the spotlight, in case she is ever revealed."

In her eyes, the logic was sound, but to Kyle he only wanted to protect and shield and love her. Their babies would be protected. Any reporter that showed up at their door, would be in for a rude awakening.

Drew nodded his head. "Well, I hate to say it man, but I kind of respect her for that. Don't you remember all the coverage of their home, the trial. The family lost everything. Then her mother committed suicide when she learned she had no money and her husband had been cheating on her all those years."

"Her families shame has not been easy on Tempe," Kyle said softly, remembering the pain on her face when she revealed her background.

"Don't you see?" Jim said. "This could be the perfect place for her. Small town, few people, working beside her husband in the clinic. Go to her. Convince her that the life you're offering would be a great hide out."

With a sigh, he shook his head remembering that terrible day. After she left, he thought of so many things he should have said, but had no way to contact her. No cell number, nothing. And yes, she'd done that on purpose.

Drew smiled. "Let's lay out your argument. First, ask her if she loves you. Did she say she loved you?"

Oh no, here came the lawyer, the attorney speak. Drew was a wonderful defender of the small guy.

"No, but Tempe is not one to let her emotions be known." Yet she had been crying when she ran out the door and he could see how hard it was for her to leave.

"She is a rather cool and collected person," Jim said. "Very logical and I admire that about her."

Drew picked up a piece of paper and started making notes. "Sorry, this is my job. First off does she love you. Second has she considered that living in a small town is the perfect hideaway. Three when she marries you, there will be another name distancing her from the Gaston name."

"So far you've said nothing new, but keep going."

"Four, who is going to search for a broke heiress in a town of less than three thousand. Five, but more importantly you love her so much that even if some reporter learns her true identity, you would protect her and your children."

For a moment, Kyle considered his brothers arguments. It was everything he had already thought of and agreed to. "But I have no way of finding her."

Laughing, Jim stood up and went to the door. "Gloria, can you come in here."

His receptionist walked into the office. "I'm sorry Kyle, but we were all worried about you."

With a flip of his hand, he blew it off. "Don't worry about calling my brothers."

With a smile at Gloria, Jim asked, "Can you tell us anything about where Tempe Tangier is at the moment."

"Oh yes, she told me she was going to the beach for a few days down in Port Aransas. The hotel she is staying at is the Sand Dollar Condominiums. Her vacation starts tomorrow."

His brothers looked at him expectedly like okay, there you go. With a sigh, he realized they were right. He had to go after her and give this one final shot.

"Brenda book me a flight to Corpus Christi."

A grin spread across her face. "Of course Dr. Lawrence. Shall I make it for one or two returning?"

At the thought of Tempe coming home with him, his heart gave an extra thump. For the first time in days, he had hope. "Let me get there first and then I'll let you know."

Turning she walked out the door humming a happy tune.

Looking at the men he loved and respected, he sighed. "Thanks guys. What if she turns me down, again?"

"We'll go get drunk somewhere," Jim said. "After Drew does his dance."

"Why would she say no to you," Drew said. "Did you offer an engagement ring the last time you asked her?"

What could he say? Last time was a desperate attempt to keep her from leaving and returning to her old life. A spur of the moment, try to hang onto her that failed miserably.

"No," he admitted. A sense of relief overcame him. "All I can do is make one more attempt. If she says no this time, it will truly be over."

"Come on, let's go spend some of your hard earned money. A man needs to do a proper proposal down on his knees, with a ring. Women expect romance. No wonder she said no," Drew exclaimed.

"Everything happened too quickly."

"Well, let's slow it down a bit and do it right."

Kyle narrowed his eyes at his youngest brother. "Fine, we will. When are you going to do the Cupid stupid dance?"

"Soon," he said. "Very soon. Someone in this family has to show you boys that love does not come about because of a statue."

CHAPTER 32

*T*empe sat in her beach chair and stared out at the families in the water. The mothers clinging to their toddlers hands, fathers splashing with the older children, neither far from the precious little ones as they constantly watched them.

Pain gripped her chest and it wasn't from the fading bruise. Oh no, this was from a broken heart. A heart that realized children, a loving husband, and her charm boy Kyle were not possible for a woman with such a public past.

Raising her book, she once again tried to read the sappy romance, but the words blurred on the page. All through college, she kept herself entertained with stories with a happy ending. But there would be no happy ending for Tempe.

Picking up her water, she drained the bottle to keep her sadness from spilling down her cheeks and then tossed it down beside her bag.

"Hey Lady, we don't allow littering on Texas beaches," a deep voice she recognized said. Tears pricked her eyelids as her heart leaped into her throat. No, no no, he couldn't be here.

Her head all but swiveled towards Kyle, wearing swim trunks, stylish sunglasses and the grin she loved. "What are you doing here? How did you find me?"

"If you decide to stand before a minister with me, then there is one thing you should understand about the staff in my office. They're terrible at keeping secrets. Don't tell them anything you don't want the whole town to learn," he said and promptly pulled out his own chair and plopped down next to her.

"Look at that ocean, isn't it beautiful," he said.

"Gloria told you where I was?" she questioned.

"Yes, she did. The woman is the sweetest gossip in town. Not like the other women who are all waiting for the two of us to return as man and wife."

The words caused her heart to skip a beat. How could she continue to fight him, when her defenses were weak? Somehow she had to remain strong.

"Kyle, this isn't funny. You know my past and the reasons why I will never get married," she said looking around to make certain no one was listening to their conversation.

"Okay, my brother Drew is a mighty fine lawyer. We'll probably use him to draw up the new legal documents for the clinic since we'll be Dr's Lawrence and Lawrence."

Her chest ached more from emotional pain than it had even from that heifer's kick. Didn't he realize how badly he was hurting her when he said these things. Everything she ever wanted was sitting beside her and to protect him she had to push him away.

"Stop it Kyle. Enough, you know I can't marry you."

Turning in his chair, he faced her, his eyes flashing defiantly. "Hear me out before you say no again. Because if you say no a second time, then I will walk away and you'll never see me again. For both of our sakes, I hope that's not what you say, but here are my arguments."

Sitting up he swung around to meet her gaze. "One, do you love me as much as I love and can't live without you?"

"Yes, I love you," she said her insides aching. "I love you so much I don't want to drag you into my shitty life."

With a nod of his head, he continued. "Two have you considered living in a small town is the perfect hideaway? Three, as my wife your name will now be Lawrence, two names removed from your maiden name. Four, who is going to go searching for a broke heiress in the middle of cow country? Five..."

Glancing at her he paused. "Look, I understand you're concerned about protecting me and our children. As your husband, no one harasses my wife. No one. I love you so much Tempe that I would move us to Africa if I thought there was a chance of someone hurting you."

He dropped to one knee and her chest all but exploded. This is what she wanted, what she'd dreamed of and Kyle was the only man for her. But...

"Marry me and let me spend the rest of our days together, showing you how much you mean to me."

Tears welled up in her eyes and she grabbed him and kissed him full on the mouth. The logical side of her repeated this was a mistake, she was putting him in jeopardy, but her heart refused to listen. Filled with love, her heart dictated what she knew she longed for. To be Kyle's wife, his partner.

With her lips she showed him what she was feeling, knowing they were making a spectacle, but she didn't care. Finally, he pulled back.

"Honey, I'm praying that means yes, but if you don't stop, these parents are going to be upset their children witnessed a man's hard on at the beach."

Extending her hand she caressed his face. "How could I say no to a proposal all laid out with the reasons why I should marry you. Tell me you're sure that you understand the depth of the publicity that I could be subject to if anyone learns who I am."

"It doesn't matter, Tempe. You're all that matters to me. The world can go to hell as long as I have you."

Reaching into his pocket, he pulled out the box and opened it. A big bright beautiful solitaire diamond sparkled at her and she gasped.

"Oh, Kyle, you picked exactly what I would have wanted."

Smiling, he kissed her again. "See we're a good match."

"Yes, charm boy, we are. There is one stipulation. No more dancing naked around that silly Cupid statue in town."

Shaking his head, he held up his hand. "Never again. No need. That fountain found the perfect woman for me to love. She was waiting for me on my door stop."

A gasp escaped her at his heartfelt words. "With no idea what awaited her. Let's get married tonight. Just you and me here on the beach."

"Let's do it." And he reached down to seal the commitment with a kiss.

❧

SOMETIMES IT'S fun to think about how a character's family life affects them. That was the case with Tempe. How would her father's actions change her life? When I started this book all I knew was that I wanted her to find a happily ever after. But good Lord, I never realized what I would learn about cow diseases. I hope you enjoyed their story. Please be sure to leave a review.

❧

Next up Drew's Story

DREW LAWRENCE KNEW his day of reckoning had come. No longer could he avoid doing the Cupid Stupid dance all because he joined in with his brothers and agreed to the bet. But he never dreamed they would lose and the idea of dancing naked around the statue to meet love was ridiculous.

Who believed this crazy superstition.

Now, here he stood in the town square, in the buff, waiting for the church clock to strike midnight, waiting to fulfill his part of the wager he made with his future brother-in-law and child-hood friend, Cody. Thank goodness, a park surrounded the God of Love, giving cover from the main street in Cupid, Texas.

"Are you ready?" his friend asked.

"I'm naked, aren't I?" Drew replied, his hands over his privates. The weather had warmed enough, he didn't have to worry about frostbite, but still, this was certifiable. As an attorney, the penalties of being caught were high.

"Remember, three laps around chanting, 'Oh Cupid statue, find me my true love.'"

"Really?" he asked, looking at his friend. "You believe this sculpture brought you and my sister together?"

"Scout's honor," Cody said.

No one could have been better for Kelsey than Cody, but he'd been told tales about the statue for years and still didn't accept a boy in a diaper managed to shoot your heart with love. Frankly, he didn't want the emotion.

"Jim and Kyle warned me you left them without clothing. Are you going to steal my stuff?" Drew asked.

A grin spread across Cody's face. "Nah, it wouldn't work a second time."

"Well, just in case. I'm prepared." Holding up his hand, he displayed his readiness. "Car keys in hand and a pair of jeans and a shirt await me inside my car. Cell phone in the car. Remember, I'm a lawyer who tries to think of all the angles."

Drew had his older brother on standby ready to race to the rescue.

"I didn't force you to make the bet. The way I recall, you guys didn't believe your little sister would fall for me."

With a shake of his head, he turned to Cody. "Like my brothers, I'm going to keep my part of the wager. Three laps and I'm out of here. To make certain the sheriff is busy, Mrs. Raffensperger's cat is once again fighting in the alley."

"Good, he'll be occupied." Cody glanced at his watch as the bells began to chime. "Time to go."

Growling at the absurdness of this humiliation because that's all it was, he took off, a ball cap covering his junk, his keys in the other hand.

"Oh, Cupid statue find me my true love, so I can put my clothes back on," Drew said, laughing.

With a sputter, the lights that normally lit up the sculpture went dark. That was odd. Drew continued running, hoping to get this over.

During his second lap, a rustling noise caused him to glance back over his shoulder as he came around the corner and slammed into a body. A female body with breasts smashed against his chest, his head snapped around.

Startled, he recognized Chloe Kilian, the preacher's daughter. "What the hell?"

"Oh no," she screeched trying to hide all her very nice curves that she obviously had kept hidden away all these years.

"What are you doing here?" he asked stunned.

With her arm across her nipples and her hand over her privates, she glared at him. "The same thing you're doing."

Chloe would believe he was running to find a lover, not to pay off a gamble. And if the superstition could possibly be true, she would be his love. That thought had him laughing out loud.

He was the last person in town who needed to do the Cupid dance. Women were drawn to him like fish to a worm. Hook, line, and sinker.

"This is not funny," she said with a hiss.

Just then he heard Cody's voice louder than normal. "Good evening, Officer Ryan. What brings you out tonight?"

"Someone called in a fake problem with Mrs. Raffensperger's cat. That pussy lost all nine lives a week ago. So, someone must be trying to keep me occupied while they dance around Cupid. Whose clothes are those?"

Drew cursed quietly. Ryan Jones, the sheriff, stood on the other side of that sculptured granite waiting to arrest whoever came around.

Even in the darkness, he saw Chloe's eyes widen with fright as she identified the sheriff's voice. Grabbing her by the arm, he mouthed the words. "Come on, let's get out of here."

Cody's stall tactics wouldn't work for long, they had to run barefoot through the wooded area.

She didn't resist as he pulled her along. They ran through the bushes, picking up scratches. Drew prayed there were no teenagers necking with their girlfriend on the swings, something he experienced as a young man learning about sexual desire. Nothing like two au naturel people streaking by to startle a kid and scar him for life.

"Where are we going," she gasped.

"If we go around the park, we'll come out close to my car."

"My clothes?"

"Forget the garments," he said. "At least for now."

Running behind him, he couldn't see much of her in the shadows which was a damn disappointment after what he witnessed near the God of Love.

The preacher's daughter's curves would be like driving a Corvette on a mountain switchback - full and exciting, rounded and dangerous.

Available at your favorite retailer!

The Bad Boy Wants The Preacher's Daughter...At Least For One Night

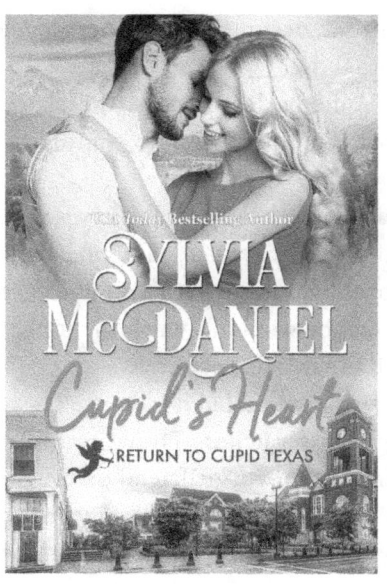

PLEASE LEAVE A REVIEW

Did you enjoy the book? Reviews help authors. I would appreciate you posting a review. Click here to leave a review.

Follow Sylvia McDaniel on Facebook.

Sign up for my New Book Alert and receive a free book.

The Burnett Brides

TRAVIS

SYLVIA McDANIEL

Travis Burnett glanced around the boardroom table at those gathered. It wasn't a fancy boardroom, but rather one filled with pictures of family members who had fought and struggled on the Burnett Ranch making it a success.

For over a century, they had worked cattle and made this outfit one of the most profitable and most lucrative in all of Texas.

Now twelve members all related to Eugenia and Thomas Burnett, who started the Burnett Ranch over one hundred years ago, sat around the table to make decisions about their commercial ranch. A dozen members who he often felt like throttling when they came before the board with their cockamamie ideas, who he knew many would disagree with his latest idea.

And still, he had to try. They had more than enough money. Why not focus on the cattle and horses? Especially now that they were talking about reality television shows coming to the dude ranch.

Not a good idea.

"Why in the world would we want to let a ghost hunting show come to the ranch?" he asked, wondering what they were thinking. Or smoking for that matter. "We don't need that kind of notoriety."

Most of the board members were in their twenties, all family with only two of the previous generation still making decisions about their corporation.

"It could draw even more attention and make us even more popular," his cousin Joshua said.

The fool must not have been visited by their great-great-great-great-grandmother. All they needed was for the television show to see her, and oh yes, they would most definitely be the most popular dude ranch in the U.S.—for all the wrong reasons.

"Have you been visited by the ghost?" Travis asked. Was he the only one of this generation who had seen her?

"You don't believe that nonsense do you?" Joshua said, his smile wide. "Come on, ghosts are not real. And if they are, we should make money on them."

"Yeah, they need to earn their keep," his cousin Cody said laughing. "We could make a lot of money on this show, and think of the free advertising."

"Think of all the looky-loos we'd get. Spend the night at the ranch and see a ghost," he said.

"She's not real," Justin said. "Eugenia Burnett Jones lives on because of her matchmaking reputation."

"How do you think your ancestors found love?" Aunt Rose asked.

"Oh, please," Jacob said. "If she was the matchmaker, why aren't you married?"

Oh, dear, that was not the way to get along with their aunt. The woman could be vindictive if she felt you were not supporting the family business the way she thought you should.

"We'll talk after this is over. I thought you would have known my story, but I'll be sure to enlighten you," she said, her face red.

That kid had a lot to learn if he wanted to stay on the board and be in Aunt Rose's good graces.

What could he say that wouldn't make him look like a fool?

And yet they needed to know. Maybe if he admitted to seeing her, others would as well.

"I've seen her," he said, not wanting to admit to it, but knowing that some apparition had visited him and told him it was past time for him to remarry. "I'll give her your name the next time she comes to visit."

The damn ghost bothered him about once a week telling him about the latest guests that she thought would be a good match for him. And so far, he'd avoided all of them.

His cousin Joshua leaned back in his chair and laughed. "I didn't think you visited the bars. Did you hold a seance like our ancestor used to do?"

"I only drink at home," he said. "And no seances were held. Just wait, she'll come visit you. Then let's talk."

The man shook his head, but everyone else at the table remained silent. They either had seen the ghost or they weren't saying. She'd been here for generations and even his father had confessed to seeing her.

"We don't need that kind of publicity," his aunt Rose said. "That could hurt our business."

The woman had never married, but rather made the ranch her permanent home and lived in the big house. Someday she would give it up, and Travis was next in line to live there.

But while the house had been remodeled, added onto, and made into a modern mansion, he would never move into the old homestead. A family needed to live in the house that had existed for over a hundred years. Since he never planned on marrying again, he would probably give it to his brother Tanner.

"Time to move on. I make a motion that we allow the ghost-hunting television show be allowed to film on the ranch," his cousin Jacob said, glancing at his brother Joshua with a grin.

"All in favor vote," Rose said. She was the head of the family and the corporation. Nothing got by this woman.

Only four of the twelve voted to allow them to film on the

ranch. Travis smiled and decided it was time for him to make his desires known. It was time they realized what a pain in the ass the dude ranch had become.

He was tired of drunken guests, crying children, people ignoring the rules, and women who only came to go shopping in Dallas. People could be a real pain in the ass and so many that were sitting around this board didn't have to deal with them.

"Motion failed," Rose said, the oldest of the family there and the head of the directors. "The next item on the agenda is from Travis."

She gazed at him like he was the biggest pain in the ass of the group, but he knew that wasn't true. That was his cousin Cameron. That boy had tried the patience of all of them with his privileged behavior. Travis had taken his Corvette keys away twice and told him if it happened a third time, he'd take the car.

No one was allowed to drive drunk and Cameron did enjoy his beer.

All of their eyes were on him, wondering what he wanted this time. And they were going to be shocked.

"I'd like to make a motion that we close the dude ranch part of the business," he said.

They all stared at him like he was crazy. Several of his cousins leaned back in their chairs and laughed. Of course, they were the ones who did not work with the people. They were the ones who didn't have to put up with some of the stunts their guests had pulled.

"Why?" Rose, who was nearing seventy, asked. "We make good money from the dude ranch."

"Because I'm tired of dealing with the crazies who come here thinking they can be vacation cowboys. Someone is going to get seriously hurt and then we'll be sued."

"We have insurance to handle that," Aunt Rose said.

Justin shook his head. Travis's father, Mark Burnett, had taken the ranch into the modern day and upgraded their operations. But still, that didn't mean they needed the dude ranch. They were all extremely rich from the family business. Almost every Burnett had over a billion dollars in the bank thanks to their hard-working ancestors, great cattle, and even a little oil money.

His cousin Caleb shook his head. The boy had graduated college with a marketing degree and his focus was on getting them as much publicity as possible with a fancy website, newsletters, and Instagram and Facebook profiles. Not to mention the money he spent on advertising.

"I'm with Rose. Our profit margin is over fifty percent. People come here and enjoy riding horses, swimming, and our cookouts. We're in almost every travel magazine in the state of Texas and I'm attending a travel show next week in Washington D.C. that will showcase us even more."

Damn, this was not going well.

"Caleb, I'm glad you've made the dude ranch a big success, but I'm the one who has to deal with entertaining our guests and making certain that our clients don't do something stupid like try to tame a bull. That happened last year."

A smile crossed his cousin's face. "And you do a fine job of it. But we spent over twenty thousand dollars to get into these travel magazines. That would be a complete waste of money. I don't like to squander money."

Shit, this wasn't going well at all.

"Maybe, Travis, you should let the workers we hire do the trail rides and even the rodeo we host," Cody Burnett, Caleb's brother said.

Now that was just pure craziness. Neither one of them had ever worked the guest angle of the dude ranch.

"You would entrust our guests' safety to hired hands? Are you willing to risk us being sued?"

His brother Tucker who had been leaning back watching the interplay between the family finally spoke up. "I'm with Travis.

Our guests need to be protected from themselves. That must always be something a family member handles. And a priority."

Oh, dear, his aunt Rose was frowning and she had that look on her face that implied you were suggesting they hire monsters. This was not someone you wanted to piss off and it appeared that Travis had just made her furious.

"The Burnett Ranch was established in 1870 right after the Civil War. My grandfather opened the dude ranch back in 1946 and saved our heritage with the money he made showing city slickers our life in the country. I'm never going to be for closing a piece of our heritage," his aunt Rose said, glaring at him like he was robbing the family silver.

The old woman had more money than any of them and no heirs.

"You're so right," his cousin Desiree said and Travis wanted to barf.

The woman worked in the front office and didn't know a thing about ranch life, though her father had been a great cowboy until an accident sidelined him. Now he sat on the board, but hardly ever said anything. He just let the younger generation make the decisions with Aunt Rose leading them.

"Any other discussion on closing the dude ranch?"

Everyone was silent.

"Let's vote," his aunt said.

There was no chance in hell this was going to pass, but he had to try for his own sanity.

"There are only three votes. The dude ranch will continue," his aunt said. "Next piece of business is the hiring of the new chef. She graduated from Escoffier in Boulder, Colorado, and is top rated."

Tanner raised his brows. "So why is she willing to come to a ranch on the outskirts of Texas? What have we got to offer? Why not some fancy-schmancy restaurant in New York?"

His aunt smiled. "Let's just say that she's had some bad things happen in her life and she needs a break from the hifalutin culinary world but wants to continue doing what she loves."

"Well, then she's not going to stay here long," Tanner said.

Travis remembered when she had flown down and toured their kitchen and cooked them a meal. The food had been excellent. Kind of frou-frou, but that's what people were expecting.

"Stop making assumptions, Tanner," Cousin Cameron said. "We don't know that. She may learn she loves Texas."

"No snow, warm winters, and hot-as-hell summers," Justin said.

Travis glanced at his brother and grinned. He'd just gotten his hand slapped by the next to youngest Burnett cousin Cameron and a smackdown from Justin. Desiree was the youngest, but that girl had a head on her shoulders.

"I make a motion that we hire her," Cousin Desiree said.

"Have we tasted her cooking?" Tucker asked.

"Yes, we had her out here a few weeks ago. You were in LA," Cody said.

That was the problem with Tucker. He had his own business to run and, oftentimes, he wasn't here when important decisions were made, though he did his best to attend every board meeting.

"Where was I?" Tanner asked.

Travis leaned over. "You were getting a checkup at the VA Hospital in Dallas," he said.

Tanner frowned and Travis knew he didn't like it when they talked about his PTSD. But the man had come so far from when he came home from the war.

"All in favor, raise your hands," his aunt said.

It was unanimous.

"She's hired. I'll have Katie send her the package offer. If all goes well, she'll be here in the next two weeks."

They all glanced around at each other knowing the board meeting was almost over and ready to get out of here. The small room was stuffy and he could hear the office staff right outside the doors keeping things running.

"I need someone to make a motion to adjourn the meeting."

His cousin Jacob spoke up and immediately they all voted on ending their once-a-month board meeting.

Once it was over, Travis slowly rose, knowing what he had to go do. It was past time and he wanted to get out there before they closed the gates.

"Gotta go," he told his family and grabbed his hat on the way out the door.

Shoving it on his head, he walked out to his truck parked not far from the office building.

Climbing in, he started up the vehicle and pulled out of the drive. As much as he hated cemeteries, he seemed to always find a sense of desolate peace when visiting.

It took him about twenty minutes to drive to the Riverdale Cemetery. When he pulled through the gate, the memory of the day of the funeral slapped him in the face.

Of standing between his brothers, staring in horror as they lowered her casket into the ground. The feeling of numbness that this couldn't be happening had overwhelmed him. In an instant, his life had changed forever.

Putting the truck in park and turning off the ignition, he reached for the flowers he'd bought and grabbed them off the seat.

As he climbed out of the truck, he glanced around at the barren place and the sense of sadness that seemed to permeate the air.

Walking up to the grave, he stared down at the tombstone. *Amanda Burnett and child. Taken Much Too Soon.*

With a sigh, he leaned down and took out the old flowers in the vase and put the new ones in. Every time he came here, his heart would ache with loneliness. Sorrow would fill his eyes with tears.

"God, how I still miss you. Our baby would be almost two years old. You two were my life and now I have nothing."

The wind blew and he heard the tinkling of wind chimes. It almost sounded like she answered him.

"I doubt you know I'm here, but still I have to come check on you. Even if I'm just staring at a piece of rock with your name on it."

Slowly he rose. "Today, I tried to convince the family to close the dude ranch, but they weren't interested. I couldn't help but think about how much you loved the talent show. Without your touch, it just never is the same. God, how do I go on living without you?"

For almost three years, he'd asked himself that same question over and over.

He sighed and glanced around at all the tombstones. His heart ached with the sadness of this lonely land. Glancing over, he saw other family members, but he never thought to bring flowers to them.

Only Amanda and their baby.

Swallowing hard, he knew he had to leave. He couldn't stay long, it hurt too much.

"Gotta go, darling. See you next time."

Turning, he hurried to the truck, jumped in, and started the vehicle.

Damn, it just wasn't fair. They had loved each other since they were sixteen and their life together had ended way too early.

Available at Your Favorite Retailer

Contemporary Romance
Burnett Brides Contemporary Times
Travis

Tanner

Tucker

Joshua

Jacob

Justin

Return to Cupid, Texas
Cupid Stupid

Cupid Scores

Cupid's Dance

Cupid Help Me!

Cupid Cures

**Cupid's Heart

Cupid Santa

**Cupid Second Chance

Cupid Charmer

Cupid Crazy

Cupid's Bachelorette

Cupid Games

Return to Cupid Box Set Books 1-3

Cupid Help Me Box Set Books 4-6

**The Unlucky Bride

Contemporary Romance
My Sister's Boyfriend

The Wanted Bride

The Reluctant Santa

The Relationship Coach

Secrets, Lies, & Online Dating

Bride, Texas Multi-Author Series
**The Unlucky Bride

Lipstick and Lead 2.0
Nailing the Hit Man
Nailing the Billionaire
Nailing the Single Dad

Secrets of Mustang Island
Secrets of a Summer Place
Secrets of a Runaway Bride
Secrets From the Past

The Langley Legacy
Collin's Challenge

Short Sexy Reads
Racy Reunions Series
Paying For the Past
Her Christmas Lie
Cupid's Revenge

Western Historicals
A Hero's Heart
Second Chance Cowboy
Ethan

American Brides
**Katie: Bride of Virginia

Angel Creek Christmas Brides
Charity
Ginger
Minnie

Cora

The Burnett Brides Series
The Rancher Takes A Bride
The Outlaw Takes A Bride
The Marshal Takes A Bride
The Christmas Bride
Boxed Set

Lipstick and Lead Series
Desperate
Deadly
Dangerous
Daring
**Determined
Deceived
Defiant
Devious
Lipstick and Lead Box Set Books 1-4
**Quinlan's Quest

Mail Order Bride Tales
**A Brother's Betrayal
**Pearl
**Ace's Bride

Scandalous Suffragettes of the West
**Abigail
Bella
Mistletoe Scandal

Southern Historical Romance
A Scarlet Bride

The Cuvier Women
Wronged
Betrayed
Beguiled
Boxed Set

** Denotes a sweet book.

Want to learn about my new releases before anyone else? Sign up for my New Book Alert and receive a free book.

USA Today Best-selling author, Sylvia McDaniel obviously has too much time on her hands. With over eighty western historical and contemporary romance novels, she spends most days torturing her characters. Bad boys deserve punishment and even good girls get into trouble. Always looking for the next plot twist, she's known for her sweet, funny, family-oriented romances.

Married to her best friend for over twenty-five years, they recently moved to the state of Colorado where they like to hike, and enjoy the beauty of the forest behind their home with their spoiled dachshund Zeus. (He has his own column in her newsletter.)

Their grown son, still lives in Texas. An avid football watcher, she loves the Broncos and the Cowboys, especially when they're winning.

www.SylviaMcDaniel.com
Sylvia@SylviaMcDaniel.com
The End!